ONE TO ~~D0327539~~

The Sioux crashed down on him, deadly knife slashing out. Slocum rolled to the side and brought his rifle up. Sparks leapt off the barrel as Slocum deflected the knife thrust. He kicked out at the Sioux to get the warrior off him. For an instant, this worked. Then Slocum grappled with the scout and tumbled forward off the boulder.

They crashed hard to the rocky ground, striving for advantage. Slocum had lost his rifle, but the brave clung fiercely to his knife. The Indian's lips pulled back in a silent, feral snarl. Then he attacked. Slocum drew his six-gun and fired point-blank into the man's belly . . .

JAKE LOGAN

SLOCUM
AND THE
VANISHED

JOVE BOOKS, NEW YORK

THE BERKLEY PUBLISHING GROUP
Published by the Penguin Group
Penguin Group (USA) Inc.
375 Hudson Street, New York, New York 10014, USA
Penguin Group (Canada), 90 Eglinton Avenue East, Suite 700, Toronto, Ontario M4P 2Y3, Canada
(a division of Pearson Penguin Canada Inc.)
Penguin Books Ltd., 80 Strand, London WC2R 0RL, England
Penguin Group Ireland, 25 St. Stephen's Green, Dublin 2, Ireland (a division of Penguin Books Ltd.)
Penguin Group (Australia), 250 Camberwell Road, Camberwell, Victoria 3124, Australia
(a division of Pearson Australia Group Pty. Ltd.)
Penguin Books India Pvt. Ltd., 11 Community Centre, Panchsheel Park, New Delhi—110 017, India
Penguin Group (NZ), Cnr. Airborne and Rosedale Roads, Albany, Auckland 1310, New Zealand
(a division of Pearson New Zealand Ltd.)
Penguin Books (South Africa) (Pty.) Ltd., 24 Sturdee Avenue, Rosebank, Johannesburg 2196,
South Africa

Penguin Books Ltd., Registered Offices: 80 Strand, London WC2R 0RL, England

This is a work of fiction. Names, characters, places, and incidents either are the product of the author's imagination or are used fictitiously, and any resemblance to actual persons, living or dead, business establishments, events, or locales is entirely coincidental.

SLOCUM AND THE VANISHED

A Jove Book / published by arrangement with the author

PRINTING HISTORY
Jove edition / November 2005

ISBN: 0-515-14029-5

JOVE®
Jove Books are published by The Berkley Publishing Group,
a division of Penguin Group (USA) Inc.,
375 Hudson Street, New York, New York 10014.
JOVE is a registered trademark of Penguin Group (USA) Inc.
The "J" design is a trademark belonging to Penguin Group (USA) Inc.

PRINTED IN THE UNITED STATES OF AMERICA

10 9 8 7 6 5 4 3 2 1

1

The Sioux war party was going to lift John Slocum's scalp unless he did something fast. The only problem was that he had tried everything he could think of to get away from the determined warriors for three solid days after he had run afoul of them at a watering hole in the middle of the Black Hills. That had been a sacred spot for the Indians, or maybe they were just pissed at him for drinking their water.

It hardly mattered what their reason might be for hating him so much. They had killed two horses, one a pack animal and the other a decently saddle-broken gelding, leaving him only an exhausted strawberry roan to get him away from their relentless pursuit. Slocum twisted in the saddle and felt the horse stagger slightly under him. Horse and rider were close to exhaustion and needed rest, but as Slocum fumbled about in his saddlebags he saw this wasn't in the cards. He had begun this deadly cat-and-mouse with more than a hundred rounds of ammunition for his trusty Winchester rifle and about half that for the Colt Navy he carried slung in a cross-draw holster. He had a dozen rounds left for the rifle and only what was loaded into the six-gun's chambers.

And still the Sioux came on, no matter that he had tried to parley with them before trying to fight them off. Whatever riled them amounted to a blood feud that wasn't going to end until they had run him to ground and killed him. Slocum was bone tired but wasn't going to give in without taking at least one of the red devils with him.

"There's a good spot to make a stand," Slocum said, trying to convince himself he might get out of this alive. He guided his horse to a crevice between two boulders, dismounted and led his balky horse through the shoulders-wide cleft into what looked like a box canyon. He went cold at the sight of the rocky walls soaring on all sides of the winding canyon leading away into even higher mountains. He wasn't going to escape this way. He had considered making a stand. Now he was forced to.

Grabbing the loose ammo from his saddlebags, he stuffed the cartridges into his jacket pocket and clambered to the top of the boulder forming the left pillar of the entrance. He flopped on his belly and sighted along the Winchester's barrel, waiting for the first sign of a Sioux brave. During the war Slocum had been a sniper for the C.S.A., and a good one, to boot. More than one Yankee officer had died because of a sudden flash of sunlight off gold braid had given Slocum a decent, unexpected target. Without a leader, an army fought poorly. He tried to convince himself that the Sioux war party would turn and go away if he figured out which of their number was the war chief and killed him.

Some Indians thought that way. But Slocum didn't know if it was true of the Lakota or other bands of Sioux roaming through the Black Hills of South Dakota and down into Nebraska where he skirted tall mountains trying in vain to reach Scott's Bluff or any other town where he might recruit a gun or two in his fight against the Indians.

It had been too much to imagine that he could reach the safety of Fort Robinson. Now Slocum only hoped to take a few of the red-skinned bastards with him and give the buzzards overhead a real feast. He wiggled around and got his six-shooter positioned at his side so he could draw it when his rifle ran empty. He had a decent field of fire down the slope back in the direction where he had been riding only a few minutes earlier. His horse whinnied and neighed in protest at being so tired and not having water. He wished it would quiet down. The Sioux were too good at tracking— they had proven that over the past three days—but some small spark of hope burned within Slocum that they might miss the last turn he had taken. The ground was rocky and didn't take kindly to hoofprints.

He saw a broken eagle feather poke up above a rock not twenty yards distant. He had seen that feather before, stuck into the greasy black hair of the Sioux scout responsible for tracking him so diligently. Slocum took a deep, calming breath and considered his options. The Sioux warrior might not know how close he was to his quarry. A quick sneak, a slash of the knife Slocum kept tucked away in his boot top might eliminate the scout. The main war party would never know what had happened.

Like hell. Slocum knew another scout and another and another would be sent out until he could no longer kill them. For all that, he wasn't certain he could quietly eliminate this scout. The feather dipped down below the top of the distant rock. Slocum estimated which way the Indian moved, then sighted in on a spot where the scout would appear. After a dozen rhythmic heartbeats and the Indian did not appear, Slocum knew he had been wrong. The scout had spotted him and was moving in the opposite direction.

Whipping the rifle around, Slocum settled it in time to get a good shot off at the brave moving on silent moccasins toward him up a draw. The hot lead missed and went ricocheting off a rock, causing a bigger racket than the rifle report echoing down the ravine.

The scout let out a whoop and signaled the main war party. Slocum fired and missed again.

He was in hot water up to his ears, and it was getting hotter by the second.

A dozen braves, all safely beyond the range of his rifle,

shook war lances in his direction and shouted curses at him. They tried to draw his fire. They didn't have to be reading his mind to know how short of ammo he was. After his pack horse had been killed, he had been running and fighting with decreasing supplies. At every turn they had tried to draw his fire and further reduce his ammunition.

Slocum settled down, took a good gander at the biggest of the braves, judged windage, then fired. He was an expert marksman but had to admit luck finally came his way. The round caught the brave in the chest, sending him crashing to the ground. From the way he kicked and thrashed about, Slocum knew he hadn't killed him, but this was the first time he had put even the smallest fear into the Sioux. The others went berserk, screaming curses and firing their rifles in his direction. Their rounds went wide, showing how difficult Slocum's shot had been.

Then he found himself occupied with the scout. Slocum cursed for being so careless, for neglecting the brave's advance. A soft slipping sound of leather across rough rock was all the warning Slocum got before his sky filled with silent fury.

The Sioux crashed down on him, deadly knife slashing out. Slocum rolled to the side and brought his rifle up. Sparks leaped off the barrel as Slocum deflected the downward knife thrust. He got one foot up and shoved it hard into the Sioux's belly, kicking hard to get the warrior off him. For an instant, this worked. Then Slocum grappled with the scout and tumbled forward off the boulder where he had set his ambush.

They crashed hard to the rocky ground, striving for advantage. Slocum had lost his rifle, but the brave clung fiercely to his knife. The Indian's lips pulled back in a silent, feral snarl. Then he attacked. Slocum drew his six-gun and fired point-blank into the man's belly.

Fire blasted through Slocum's arm and the warm flood of his blood quickly followed. But the scout lay dead on the ground at his feet. Slocum tried to lift his left arm and couldn't. The knife had barely missed his heart, sliding between his chest and left arm. The sharp knife tip had opened a gash on the inside of his arm.

Slocum swung about, lifted his Colt Navy and emptied it at the charging Sioux warriors. He didn't hit any of them but managed to turn their attack. For a few seconds.

Leaving the dead Sioux scout, Slocum scrambled back to the top of the boulder and grabbed his rifle. Lifting it to his shoulder proved difficult as his left arm refused to support the weapon properly. His hand shook, and the steady flow of blood made Slocum giddy.

He got off a round but saw that the Sioux smelled his wound, his weakness, and were not going to flee this time. They charged straight up the path at him—and all he had was a few rounds in the rifle. With his left arm almost useless, he needed too much time to reload the magazine.

Slocum fired again. Then he wondered at the thunder rolling all around him. The Sioux had to be firing their rifles as fast as they could pull their triggers, yet no lead sang around him. He wiped sweat from his eyes and saw the Sioux racing back the way they had come.

"Get down, you damn fool!" came a loud command. "You want yer head blowed off?"

Slocum flopped down on the rock and clumsily worked the lever on his rifle. His left arm hurt like hell now, but he had gotten a respite from the Indian attack and wasn't going to pass up whatever cards were being dealt.

As he lay waiting, his trigger finger tense, he saw the flash of blue uniforms. During the war he had shot at soldiers dressed like this. Now he heaved a sigh of heartfelt relief. The cavalry had come to him rather than him going to their fort for help.

The squad made their way onto the trail from either side. Slocum did a quick count and reckoned there were at least ten troopers. He had hoped for an entire regiment, but even this paltry number was going to let him get out alive.

"You got a horse?" called a sergeant.

"It's exhausted. It can hardly stand. The Sioux have chased me for three days." Slocum saw the non-com's disbelief at this. The sergeant shrugged it off.

"Get the horse. We can't hold 'em too long."

"Are there other soldiers or is it just your squad?" asked Slocum, painfully sliding down the rock. He hit the ground hard and his knees buckled. Slocum forced himself back upright.

The sergeant rode over and saw the dead Sioux scout, then stared hard at Slocum. The non-com had light blue eyes and hair so black it might have been colored with coal dust. In spite of a tan, there was a paleness to him that hinted at more hours spent indoors rather than under the burning Nebraska prairie sun.

"I do declare, there might be more to you than meets the eye. But there'll be a lot less if you don't get your nag into a gallop. There's no way my men can hold off that war party."

"What's got the Sioux so riled?" Slocum asked. He walked with as sure a step as he could, rounding the boulder and finding his roan nervously tugging at grass. The horse looked up at him, whites rimming its eyes, showing how fear and exhaustion still held its usual high spirits in check.

"Who knows? Sometimes it's a miner on what they call their sacred land. This time?" The sergeant shrugged expressively.

"You from New Orleans?" Slocum asked as he dragged himself into the saddle again. It took almost all his strength. The arm wound had clotted and no longer soaked his clothing with fresh blood, but he had weakened to the point he might fall out of the saddle if he didn't pay attention.

"Guilty," the sergeant said. "Name's Thibadeaux and we can exchange pleasantries later."

"You from Fort Robinson?"

"None other than," Sergeant Thibadeaux said. "Now quit jawing and start riding."

They had hardly gone a dozen yards back to the tight knot of soldiers standing guard on the trail when the Sioux opened fire and attacked with a ferocity that made Slocum wonder at their ire. On his left a soldier gasped and clutched his thigh. A Sioux bullet had ripped a chunk of flesh off his leg. In spite of his own dizziness, Slocum reached out and grabbed the private to keep him from tumbling to the ground.

"Thanks," the soldier grated out. "You look worse 'n me."

"We're all in this together," Slocum said, reverting to his old habits of command. He knew when he saw a soldier on the verge of giving up. As a captain, Slocum had spent too much time bolstering the spirits of his troops and convincing them they were part of a larger group that depended on their skill and bravery.

"You jist ride 'hind me. We're gonna get outta here," the private said. "The Sarge, he's a good man. Won't let them redskins out-soldier us, no sir."

Those were the man's last words. A Sioux war lance whistled through the air and impaled the private. He fell bonelessly from his horse. Slocum never hesitated. Grabbing the other horse's bridle, he pulled it closer and traded mounts. His roan heaved a shuddery sigh of relief at no longer having Slocum astride.

"We can't fight them," Thibadeaux said. "We have to hightail it. You up to that?"

Slocum marvelled at the persistence and ferocity of the Sioux war party.

"Lead the way, or do you want me to?"

Thibadeaux laughed and shook his head.

"You're the civilian, we're the U.S. Army. Ride behind me. Buy me a cognac when we get to the fort."

"I'll buy you a damned bottle," Slocum promised.

Sergeant Thibadeaux was already shouting orders to his remaining men. He glanced down at the fallen private. Slocum knew what troubled the sergeant. Leaving a body behind invited the Indians to mutilate it, but if they took the

time to sling it over a horse—the one Slocum rode now—
they might join the private in hell.

"Squad, f'waaard!" cried Thibadeaux. He pulled out his
service pistol and began firing as he led the wild charge
down the trail. Slocum would have added the power of his
own six-gun to the fusillade but he had already emptied it.
There was no way he could ride and fire the private's still-
sheathed carbine with his left arm flopping about uselessly.
He put his head down and concentrated on remaining
astride the horse.

And for almost a mile Slocum thought they had reached
freedom. They burst out of the rocky foothills and onto the
more level prairie. This exposed the Sioux, but it also
worked against the soldiers. There was nowhere to stand
and fight when Sergeant Thibadeaux's horse stepped into a
prairie dog hole and broke its leg.

"Go on, get on out of here. Find the captain. Get the
whole damn company back here on the double!" The sergeant pushed himself up on one elbow and shook his fist
at the others in his squad. "Get on out of here! Obey the
order!"

"We cain't let you stay and git yerse'f kilt," protested a
trooper. The soldier looked uneasily along their back trail
at the approaching war party.

"We'll all get killed if you don't get reinforcements,"
Thibadeaux said.

"Go on," Slocum said. "I'll stay here with the sergeant."
Slocum had seen what the other soldiers hadn't. When
Thibadeaux was thrown from his horse, he had broken his
right leg. The sergeant wasn't going to ride anytime soon.

"Leave us a couple carbines. And get the captain!"

Seeing that Slocum was willing to stay let the others off
the hook. The private dragged out his carbine and tossed it
to Slocum, who awkwardly caught it. Pain driving into his
shoulder, Slocum hefted the short rifle and turned to sight
in on the rapidly approaching Indians. He squeezed off a
shot. The recoil staggered him, but he had shot the horse out

from under the leading Sioux brave. This, as much as any-thing else, convinced the soldiers to obey their sergeant.

"You can join 'em," Thibadeaux said, wincing in pain now that his squad was gone. "We're going to die out here."

"You saved me earlier. Might be it was only a postpone-ment, but we both need to stick around long enough to sample that cognac."

"Fort Robinson cognac," scoffed Thibadeaux. "It's homemade. Not been within five thousand miles of France." The sergeant rolled over, got a carbine into posi-tion and began slow, methodical fire that caused the Sioux to rethink their attack.

"They won't take long to circle us," Slocum said.

"Wish I had a taste of even ole Leo's fake cognac right about now. It'd make dying a sight easier."

"We're not dead yet," Slocum said. He balanced his rifle against a rock as he lay prone, peering through the tall grass fitfully swaying in the late afternoon breeze. When he got a target, he fired. And missed. But the lead streaking past the brave's ear forced him to reconsider approaching on horseback.

"They're going to ground and will sneak up on us where we can't see them," Thibadeaux said. "I've seen them do this time and again. Only way to fight that tactic is to mount up and ride like the wind."

Slocum saw the ugly white bone jutting from the sergeant's thigh. Such a bad break needed immediate at-tention by a doctor. Even then there might not be any way to save the man's leg. Fighting simply to stay alive cut their chances for such attention. But Slocum owed the sergeant and wasn't inclined to abandon him to the Indians.

"My name's Slocum."

"Pierre Thibadeaux," the sergeant said, thrusting out a long-fingered, almost delicate hand. The heavy calluses belied the slender bone structure. "Nobody calls me that. Pete's the moniker out here." Thibadeaux took time to fire three quick rounds before settling back.

"They're coming at us from the south now," Slocum said, head cocked to one side.

"You've got good ears. Or you guess real good. Either way, sorry I can't hire you as a scout. We lost the Blackfoot we had at Fort Robinson. He either ran off or got killed. Never knew which."

Before Slocum could say anything more he found himself engaged in a short, brief exchange with two Sioux braves who suddenly appeared amid the knee-high grass. He clumsily fired, discarded the carbine and picked up another left by the fleeing soldiers.

"You hear that?" asked Slocum. "Hoofbeats. Lots of them."

"What do you figure that means?" asked Thibadeaux.

"We're either in a whale of a lot of trouble or your squad found the rest of the company," said Slocum. He hardly dared hope the rest of the cavalry unit was so close. He fired twice more, missing both times as the Indians popped up like prairie dogs, then ducked back after drawing his fire. They worked to exhaust his ammunition—and it was working. Slocum thought he had fewer than a half dozen rounds left. Unless the cavalry came at a gallop, he and Thibadeaux were in deep trouble.

"Why don't they run off?" wondered Thibadeaux aloud. "Even I can hear the horses now, and I'm damned near deaf in one ear. They're persistent cusses, aren't they?"

Slocum heard a curious gurgling sound and turned to look at the sergeant. A Sioux had crept within a few feet of the non-com without him knowing. The Indian might have come up on the sergeant's deaf side or just been skillful. The quick slash from a knife had left Thibadeaux with a bloody throat.

Slocum fired but the dull *snap!* told him the hammer had fallen on a dud. Wincing with pain, he rolled over and swung his rifle like a club and connected squarely with the side of the Indian's head, knocking the brave backward. Slocum dropped his carbine and grabbed for the knife sheathed in his boot. Before the Sioux shook off the effects of being buffaloed by an Army carbine, Slocum dispatched him.

Then he saw the grass all around begin to sway and churn, as if a dozen slithering creatures made their way toward him. He knew the Sioux were ready to charge. He gripped his knife and waited for an attack that never came.

"The Indians are leaving," Slocum told Thibadeaux. The sergeant stared up at him with pain-wracked eyes. He clutched at his bloody throat but could not stanch the flow. His lifeblood leaked around his numb fingers and ran down his arm, soaking his blue wool uniform until it turned to a gory shroud.

"Got me. I'm done for," Thibadeaux croaked out. "You got to do something for me, Slocum. Promise."

"What is it?"

"At the fort. Family Bible. Get it to my sister, Antoinette. Please." Thibadeaux shuddered and his eyes rolled up in his head. Slocum was left holding the dead man's head in his lap. As he looked up he saw a ring of blue uniformed riders.

The cavalry had arrived. Too late for Pierre Thibadeaux.

2

Slocum stood to one side, eyes closed as the rifles fired and filled the air with acrid gun smoke. He heaved a sigh and looked out across the cemetery. There were too many small whitewashed crosses in this boneyard, and a new grave yawned at the edge of endless, barren prairie. At its head was a fresh cross with Pierre Thibadeaux's name on it. The honor squad lowered their rifles after the brief salute and the post commander said a few words. Slocum might have listened, but he had heard similar sentiments too many times. He was already walking from the grave by the time four privates worked to lower the pine box and begin shoveling dirt on Thibadeaux's final resting place.

"Pardon me," Slocum called. "Captain Dawson?"

The officer who had rescued Slocum on the prairie turned bloodshot eyes toward him. For a moment Slocum thought Dawson was going to draw his sidearm and shoot him where he stood. In a way, Slocum understood the animosity. A good sergeant had died, apparently protecting a civilian who shouldn't have been riding across territory filled with hostiles.

"What?"

"The sergeant had a last request. He wanted me to send his effects to his sister, but I don't know where she is."

"Not on this post," Captain Dawson said curtly.

"Would his service records show next of kin? Thibadeaux was insistent that I get one item in particular to her."

"What was that?"

"His family's Bible." Slocum saw the officer's expression soften. He might have thought Slocum intended to steal what he could of the sergeant's belongings. Nobody stole a Bible.

"Tell Corporal Grasso I authorized you to look at the records. The sergeant mentioned her a few times. I think she's in some town between here and Scott's Bluff."

"Thank you, Captain," Slocum said. The officer executed a precise about-face and marched off as if he were on a parade ground passing in review, muttering to himself. From all Slocum had seen of Fort Robinson, they were chronically undermanned and lacked decent supply lines to keep the soldiers equipped with carbines, blankets and other necessary supplies. The armory wasn't even guarded, telling Slocum there was nothing inside worth stealing. Whatever ammunition and weapons were on the post were already in the hands of the soldiers in their barracks. Such possession by the soldiers was usually a prescription for disaster—unless the troopers needed instant access to their carbines and six-shooters. Trouble brewed in northwestern Nebraska and Slocum was going to be glad to move on and leave it behind.

He turned so the hot sun was in his face. Twitching a little, he got his left arm repositioned so it was more comfortable in its sling. The post doctor had been sober enough to do a fair job patching him up—and had somewhat grudgingly shared a few shots of rye from a personal bottle. The whiskey, as much as the doctoring, had sharpened Slocum's senses and made him feel better.

He passed the post commander's office when he saw a small sign on the building immediately to the north: REC-ORDS. Slocum went into the small, hot, cramped single room and saw a bespectacled corporal poring over a sheet of paper as if it were the most important document in the world. For all Slocum knew, it might be. But he doubted it. His experience with the military had shown him repeatedly how much paper was produced had little to do with how effective and efficient the soldiers were.

"Captain Dawson told me I could take a gander at Pierre Thibadeaux's records so I could send his effects to his sister," Slocum said.

The nearsighted corporal looked up, startled.

"Sorry, didn't hear you come in." Corporal Grasso hastily slipped the paper into the top drawer of his desk. "Now. What did you need? The sergeant's next of kin?"

"Her name's Antoinette and she lives somewhere outside of Scott's Bluff," Slocum said.

"Hmm, yes. Agate. That's to the northwest of Scott's Bluff."

"Is her last name the same as the sergeant's? Thibadeaux?"

"Why, yes," the corporal said. "I thought you knew her, and that's why you're in charge of handling this matter."

"I promised a dying man I'd see that his family Bible got into his sister's hands. I'd never laid eyes on Thibadeaux before he and his squad saved me from the Sioux war party."

"Oh," Corporal Grasso said, peering closely at Slocum. "You said the captain authorized it?" When Slocum nodded, the corporal hastily scribbled a few lines on a scrap of paper and said, "That's her. Antoinette Thibadeaux in Agate, Nebraska. Don't have more of an address, but I don't reckon you need more. Not like Agate's that big."

"Thanks," Slocum said. He stood his ground.

"What more can I do for you?"

"His effects. They weren't in his footlocker."

"Sorry about that. I've got so much on my mind." The corporal fished under his uniform jacket and pulled out a small key, swung around in his chair and began working on a lockbox to the side of his desk. Slocum could have ripped the lid off faster than it took the corporal to open the small safe. Corporal Grasso dropped a large envelope on the desk and pushed across a form for Slocum to sign.

"That's to say you took custody of the sergeant's belongings," the corporal explained.

Slocum signed and hefted the envelope, opened it and saw a fancy leather-bound Bible inside. He ran his fingers over the soft cover and lingered on the lettering. Gold. A quick riffle through the pages showed the Thibadeaux family tree, notes about relatives and other information Slocum didn't bother reading. He nodded to the corporal and stepped out into the hot Nebraska afternoon.

He had no desire to ride his broken-down roan to Agate and present the Bible to Antoinette Thibadeaux personally, but Slocum saw a way around it. He hurried to the post sutler and went inside.

"Good afternoon, mister," the clerk said, looking up from a newspaper he read. Slocum deciphered the name although it was upside down. It was a week-old Omaha newspaper.

"How do you get supplies shipped in?" Slocum asked.

The clerk shrugged and said, "They sorta trickle in, whenever a mule skinner's willing to make the trip. Don't see many these days. Whole lot of road agents in these parts, not to mention the Indians. But you know all 'bout them firsthand, don't you?"

"Reckon I do," Slocum said. "Can you handle U.S. mail from this post?"

The clerk snorted in disgust.

"We may be perched on the edge of nowhere but the mail comes through here all the time. Even got a Butterfield stage what makes a stop here three times a week."

"I have a package to mail to someone in Agate. How long would it take to arrive there?"

"Agate? That dinky place south of here?" The clerk scratched his stubbled chin and shook his head. "Can't rightly say, but not more 'n a couple weeks. If the stagecoach that's comin' through this afternoon's goin' in that direction, might not even be a week."

Slocum bought a hammer and some nails, used wood he found out behind the sutler's and clumsily put together a box for Thibadeaux's belongings. He finally drew his left arm out of the sling and tested it by stretching slowly. The muscle along the underside of his left arm gave him a twinge or two but nothing he couldn't tolerate. If anything, building the crate helped, even if it did tire out the muscles in his arm.

He lugged the crate around to the porch in front of the sutler's and sat on it, tuckered out from the work. The loss of blood had taken its toll on him. As much as Slocum wanted to see the Bible delivered into the hands of Thibadeaux's sister, sending it to her would be easier. It gave Slocum the chance to rest up another day or two and then be on his way without having to detour south toward Scott's Bluff. The town had seemed a sanctuary to him when the Sioux were hot on his trail but not now. He wanted to push directly west and get to the Oregon coast. Might be he could find a sturdy Appaloosa to replace the strawberry roan.

His mental wandering came to an abrupt halt when he heard the stagecoach rattling through the gate at the far end of the parade ground. Fort Robinson was surrounded not by a palisade but a low rail fence designed more to keep the poultry in than the Indians out. At every corner of the fence sentries walked their lonely guard routes and from a tower near the commander's office a lookout scanned the horizon with field glasses. These guards provided better protection than a tall fence might.

"Whoa, you consarned nags!" shouted the stage driver. He jumped to his feet and slammed one foot against the brake, bringing the heavy stagecoach to a halt amid a cloud of dust. With a quick whirl of the leather reins, he secured the brake and leaped to the ground, creating a new cloud of dust off his clothing. Being a stagecoach driver was dusty work.

"Howdy," the driver greeted Slocum, taking off his hat and swatting it a few times against his leg. New dust rose and settled. "You jist settin' there or you got somethin' to load onto the coach?"

"An important delivery for someone in Agate. You heading that way?"

"Sure as rain," the driver said, then peered up at the cloudless blue sky. "Make that sure as death and taxes. Ain't rained here in a month of Sundays."

"Miss Antoinette Thibadeaux," Slocum said. "She's the one to get the crate."

"Did you say Thibadeaux? That ole Pete's kin?" The driver looked as if he had lost his best friend when Slocum explained what had happened and why he had to deliver the sergeant's belongings to his sister.

"That's a danged shame," the driver said, shaking his head. "I liked ole Pete better 'n 'bout any of these horse soldiers. He had a sense of humor and was always quick to share a nip of his special firewater."

"His cognac," Slocum said.

"That's what he called it. Don't reckon there's a bottle of it in there, is there?"

Slocum suspected the corporal or some of Thibadeaux's bunkmates had already appropriated the liquor.

"Only his Bible and a few odds and ends."

"Fer ole Pete, I'd deliver it, no matter what." The driver cleared his throat and said, "'Course, that's jist me talkin'. The boss'd want ten dollars fer proper delivery or he'd have my hide tanned and hung out on the shed."

The driver looked as if his hide had already been tanned, but Slocum said nothing. He owed Thibadeaux his life. Ten dollars, even if it was more than half of all the money he had riding in his shirt pocket, was a small price to pay.

"I'll see that Miss Antoinette gets her brother's belongin's," the driver promised. "You ain't headin' that way? You need a ticket?"

"I'm going somewhere else, but in a day or two." Slocum tried to lift his arm to show his condition and found the arm refused to budge. He had worn it out building the crate.

"Well, now, mister, you jist recover and trust Zeke Maharis with droppin' off this box o' valuables. A Bible in there, you say?"

Slocum suspected the driver might open the crate and paw through it no matter what he said, but he nodded.

"A Bible and a few other things. A belt buckle, a few pictures in the Bible, family things."

This satisfied Zeke. He took Slocum's money, then heaved the crate into the boot, covering it with a tattered canvas before going into the sutler's. Slocum heard Zeke and the clerk swapping lies and suspected the clerk kept a bottle or two of tarantula juice handy for important visitors like Zeke Maharis. Slocum considered going in and sampling some of the devil's brew but found himself too tired. He made his way to the livery where he had stabled his horse and stretched out his own bedroll. Slocum intended to take a quick nap, nothing more, but the next thing he knew a ruckus outside awoke him.

He rubbed sleep from his eyes and stretched, wondering how he had gotten so stiff in only a few minutes. Then he realized the sun slanted in from the opposite direction. He had slept through the afternoon and all night, not even waking for the reveille. A quick check of his watch showed him it was after ten o'clock in the morning.

Curious, he poked his head out and looked around. The soldiers had rushed out and crowded around a solitary rider. It took Slocum a few seconds to realize the rider was a soldier but without a garrison cap. He looked as if he had been dragged through a knothole backwards.

He joined the crowd in time to hear the scout report to Captain Dawson.

"Ambushed. Just like the others. I seen 'em headin' for the Black Hills, goin' due north, sir."

"Mount up. Companies G and K, mount up. Sergeants, prepare for a weeklong sortie."

"What happened?" Slocum asked the scout, still trying to catch his breath.

"Them road agents. They're bold ones. But this time we'll get 'em. No more thievin' for them."

"What happened?" Slocum repeated more sharply.

"They robbed the stagecoach, that's what happened. Kilt Zeke and left his carcass for the coyotes."

"They robbed the stage?" Slocum fought to shake off the numbness he felt. Part of it came from being awakened and the rest from his weakness after losing so much blood. "Where? Where'd it happen?"

"Twelve, fifteen miles down the road toward Scott's Bluff, that's where. But them outlaws ain't stickin' around. I spotted them makin' for their hideout. We find it, we'll bring real justice to this country."

A sergeant bellowed at the scout and the man hastily left Slocum alone in the middle of the parade ground. In less than ten minutes, the two companies were mounted and trotting from Fort Robinson in orderly rows. Slocum watched them go in pursuit of the owlhoots who had killed Zeke Maharis, but something more ate away at his gut. He didn't wish Zeke ill. He had taken a shine to the crusty stagecoach driver, but if the stage had been robbed that meant Antoinette Thibadeaux's legacy from her brother might have been stolen.

Slocum smiled ruefully as he returned to the stables to saddle his horse and go investigate on his own. He was jumping at shadows. What road agent would steal a Bible if there was gold or other valuables aboard the stage? Even a holy book as fine as the one Thibadeaux had entreated him to deliver wasn't likely to be carried off by an outlaw.

As he rode, following the route taken by the stagecoach the evening before, Slocum became more confident that he would find the Bible and other items sent to Antoinette Thibadeaux. Nothing in the crate would have been worth stealing since it was all of sentimental, not material, value.

He kept a sharp eye out for any trace of the Sioux war party, but the prairie stretched out lonely and peaceful, as far as he could see. As the road twisted about and headed toward the southwest he entered hillier country. His sharp eyes spotted the places where Zeke had to use his whip to get the horses pulling hard up the steeper inclines. Eventually he came to a place where a dozen or more horses had churned up the road. Slocum's heart beat a little faster at the sight.

This was where the road agents had waited.

Not a quarter mile farther down the road he saw the large stagecoach tipped over on its side. From the way the buzzards circled above, he knew he had an unpleasant chore ahead of him. The scout from the post had not taken the time to bury Zeke but had rushed back to report the robbery.

Slocum dismounted and walked slowly toward the wreckage. His hand drifted toward the ebony handle of his Colt resting in its cross-draw holster as he approached. A scrawny coyote poked its gray head around the side of the coach and snarled at him. Slocum knelt, picked up a rock and heaved it at the hungry animal. Why waste good ammunition on it when he had spent almost his last dollar at the post sutler and had gotten only thirty rounds?

The coyote let out a yip and hightailed it through the tall grass, disappearing like some gray ghost. Slocum approached the front of the coach and saw that the leather reins had snapped, setting the team free when the coach had taken its tumble. Where those horses might be now was anyone's guess. Probably feed for even hungrier coyotes and wolves.

Slocum stared at what was left of Zeke Maharis and silently cursed the scout. Catching the owlhoots responsible for the robbery and the driver's death was important, but it wouldn't have taken that much longer to either return to the post with the body or cover it with enough rocks to keep away the coyotes.

Slocum had seen worse, but that didn't mean he cottoned much to the chore. He began digging in the hard prairie, using a wood stave that had been broken from the coach. Twenty minutes later, he had Zeke in a grave topped with fist-sized rocks to frustrate the scavengers. Only then did Slocum hunt for the wooden crate he had fashioned with his own hands to carry the Thibadeaux Bible.

He grinned ear to ear when he spotted the crate some distance from the coach where it had been thrown free. Slocum pictured it in his mind. Zeke trying in vain to escape. The outlaws shooting at him. The heavy stagecoach losing a wheel and rolling down this short embankment, throwing Zeke from the driver's box and the crate out of the boot.

The smile faded as Slocum got closer. The box only looked intact. The top had been yanked off and then the crate had been dropped to conceal the crime. He kicked it over and went cold inside. The crate was empty.

The outlaws had stolen Pierre Thibadeaux's Bible along with whatever else they could take from the stagecoach.

3

Slocum poked around the robbery site a while longer, finding the mailbag cut open and the contents spilled out. The road agents had hastily gone through the letters and then consigned what they didn't want to the humid Nebraska prairie wind. Of a strongbox Slocum found no trace, and he had noticed that Zeke's pockets had been turned inside out. The robbers had made sure they stole every last nickel.

After making one last circuit of the upended stagecoach and finding nothing worth mentioning, Slocum climbed into the saddle. His roan complained mightily but started on the road, going in the direction the stage had headed. Slocum had no choice but to find Antoinette Thibadeaux and tell her how her brother's legacy had been stolen.

Two days later, tired from riding but feeling better and able to throw away the sling for his left arm, Slocum rode into Agate, Nebraska. The town looked like every other prairie town he had ever seen. Some wood had come from the hills to the west and north but most of the buildings had been constructed of brick. The treeless plains forced builders to fall into tried and true patterns that wore on Slocum quickly. He lifted his gaze to the west and Wyoming. As soon as he forded the Niobrara River and got

to Agate, he would keep riding. He had seen enough flat-
land and needed mountains, real mountains.

The river proved easily forded, hardly reaching his
roan's fetlocks. The drought had taken its toll on the river,
fed from the Hat Creek Breaks. This was all the more reason for Slocum to leave the sere grasslands and find cooler
high country.

The buildings rose on either side as he rode down
Agate's main street. He noted that the town marshal neglected his job; a dead horse drew flies in the street near a
saloon and gophers had turned the street into a dangerous
area to ride a horse. Still, the quiet town looked friendly
enough and Slocum had seen worse. It was just that he
dreaded meeting Antoinette Thibadeaux and telling her
how her Bible had been stolen.

He dismounted and went into the marshal's office. It
was hot outside. Inside the jailhouse it was even hotter.
Slocum felt as if he had walked into a furnace and had to
mop at sweat threatening to blind him.

The marshal was a thin man with a frightened face.

"What kin I do fer ya?" the lawman asked.

"I have a message for Miss Thibadeaux. Antoinette
Thibadeaux. You know where I can find her?"

"What sort of message might this be?" asked the marshal. His eyes narrowed and made him look like a weasel.
His hair was plastered to his head by sweat and a weedy
mustache drooped in the heat.

"Personal," Slocum said. "Where can I find her?"

"She's the schoolmarm." The marshal laughed at some
secret joke. "She's also the town doctor and lawyer and
'bout anything else we need."

"A jack of all trades."

"Jill of all trades," the marshal corrected. "You know
her by sight?"

"I knew her brother. Sergeant Pierre Thibadeaux."

"Pierre? Oh, that must be the Pete she's always goin' on
about. Well," the marshal said, taking out his pocket watch

and peering at it, as if figuring out how to tell time, "she ought to be done with school. Don't run much in the afternoon, when the kids got chores. That means she might be over at the doctor's office."

Slocum nodded and left before the marshal could ramble on. Finding the doctor's surgery in such a small town couldn't be that difficult. He wandered about awhile, getting the feel of Agate, then spotted a neatly painted sign swinging in the fitful wind pointing to the doctor's office.

Slocum stepped inside and stopped dead in his tracks. He hadn't been sure what Antoinette would be like, but this wasn't it. She had wild black hair and eyes so blue they were fathomless, lucid pools. Her pale oval face reminded him a little of her brother, especially with its almost-fragile aspect. But Antoinette Thibadeaux was nothing short of gorgeous, with a shapely figure that would be the envy of any woman.

"May I help you?" she asked.

"Ma'am, my name's John Slocum. And I've got some bad news to pass along."

"Looks as if you've been injured."

"What?" It took Slocum a second to realize she had spotted the blood on his shirt and jacket and how his left arm still moved stiffly.

"That's nothing, ma'am. About healed. The doctor at Fort Robinson patched me up."

"Fort Robinson?"

"I just came from there," Slocum said. "Your brother had told me to see that you got the Thibadeaux family Bible. I sent it on the stagecoach, but the stage was robbed."

"I'm confused, Mr. Slocum. Why'd Pierre want *you* to see that I got the Bible?"

"He saved my life and I promised him I'd do it. I ought to have brought the Bible myself, but I didn't. I'll see what I can do to get it back from the road agents who took it."

"Now I am really confused. Pierre said he'd pass along

the Bible to his children, when he got married and had a few. He'd never send it to me." Antoinette's eyes went wide and her hand, so like her brother's, went to her mouth. "No. No, tell me it's not so."

Slocum silently cursed his bad luck. He had thought the Army had already notified Antoinette of her brother's death. He knew now that she was hearing the news for the first time—and he was the unexpected messenger.

"I thought you knew. I'm sorry. He died saving my life."

"The road agents?"

"A Sioux war party," Slocum said. He saw the woman's growing confusion. "Let me start at the beginning. I'm sorry if this is the first time you've heard any of this." He launched into a description of how her brother had saved him and detailed the sergeant's gallant death, trying to keep it as free of bloody description as possible. Slocum damned the Fort Robinson commander for not notifying Antoinette but kept on through his own mistake in trusting the Bible to the mail when road agents preyed on ship ments throughout northwestern Nebraska.

"I had no idea the robberies were so widespread," Slocum said. "I only wanted to get the Bible to you as quick as possible." He lifted his arm and started to excuse himself because of recovering from the wound, then let it drop. Thibadeaux had entrusted him with delivering the Bible, and he had failed. That put an obligation on Slocum's head he would rather not meet—but honor dictated that he had no choice. Why the road agents had taken the Bible was beyond him, but he would get it back from them.

He owed it to Pierre Thibadeaux.

"It's not your fault. You don't have to live with the . . . unrest." Antoinette dabbed at tears welling in her eyes. She smiled weakly. "I'm sorry to be like this, but Pete was all the family I had. Our ma and pa died of cholera in New Orleans and our two sisters—well, we don't talk about them much."

"You don't have to explain. Looks like you've made a good life for yourself here in Agate. I talked to the marshal, and he spoke highly of you."

"That old turd?" Antoinette laughed at Slocum's expression. "He is a total waste as lawman. He's part of the problem. He refuses to go after the gang of road agents when they rob anyone close to Agate."

"You've got classes to teach and patients to tend," Slocum said. His mind tumbled and roiled with plans. He could return to the wrecked stagecoach and follow the highwaymen from there. There might be better trackers in Nebraska, but he doubted it.

Then Slocum smiled ruefully. He had come across at least one tracker who'd been better. The Sioux scout had not been thrown off the trail once after the war party had gone after Slocum.

"I don't think I'm up to teaching, not for a while. Those children are an unruly bunch and have little interest in book learning."

"I'll be on my way, ma'am," Slocum said. He was surprised at how quickly she came to him, reached out and gently took his left arm. Even with such a light touch, he couldn't keep from wincing.

"You need that looked after. I was a nurse during the cholera epidemic that took my parents and learned a considerable amount of doctoring. If that quack at Fort Robinson treated you, you're lucky you're not dead. Pete told me some of the terrible things that so-called doctor did."

"He was fond of sampling his anesthetic," Slocum allowed. His first thought when he had seen the post doctor was that the man wasn't drunk yet. The doctor had smelled of booze, but his hands had been steady and his work adequate.

But that man's bedside manner was nothing like Antoinette's. She carefully drew the sleeve away and helped Slocum out of his shirt. Her palm rested warmly in the middle of his chest as she bent over and peered at the stitches the doctor had taken in Slocum's triceps. She seemed unaware of how her touch, her closeness, her beauty affected him. Slocum swallowed hard and tried to think of her as nothing more than a disinterested doctor.

He couldn't. The sight of the way her breasts filled her crisp white blouse, straining the buttons almost to the breaking point, was more obvious as she bent over. He stared at the warm, milky mounds and felt guilty.

"There's a touch of infection. Nothing to worry about now, but if it's not treated you might find yourself running a nasty fever in a few days." Antoinette stood and looked up at him. His green eyes locked on her bright azure ones for an instant, then she turned away.

Slocum took a deep breath and tried to push her scent, her nearness, the stark warmth of the beautiful woman's touch from his mind. That determination faded fast when she bent over to get a bottle of disinfectant from the bottom shelf of a cabinet. Antoinette's pert, perky rump poked up invitingly into the air. She waggled it a mite and did not move from her position.

"Well?" she asked.

"What?"

"I can stand like this only so long before I begin to feel stupid. I don't want to feel stupid. I want to feel . . . needed."

"I don't understand," Slocum said, but he did. Taking advantage of the woman in her grief was the last thing he wanted to do, but she obviously had an intent that he shared. He stepped forward, got a double handful of skirt and lifted slowly. If he had gotten the wrong message from her, she would let him know now, in no uncertain terms.

The farther he lifted her skirts, the more heavily she breathed. Her body quaked like an aspen leaf in a gentle mountain breeze. When he ran his fingertips over her sleek, rounded hindquarters, the dark-haired woman put her hands on the sturdy cabinet shelf to brace herself.

Slocum tugged and got her frilly undergarment pulled

down around her ankles, partially hog-tying her. She began to make tiny sounds of pleasure when he stroked the inside of her thigh and worked higher, moving with great deliberation. There was no hurry and he enjoyed the heat radiating from her body, the flow of her strong thigh muscles, the way she rotated her hips as he worked ever upward. When he touched the raven-furred triangle between her legs, she sagged a bit in reaction.

"You're wrong," Slocum said.

"What's that? No, you can't stop now. It's not wrong. It's what I want. It's what you want. Isn't it?"

Slocum almost laughed at her response.

"You were wrong about the fever. I've got it bad. And you're the one giving it to me."

"No, no, give it to *me*!" She reached back between her legs and grabbed for his crotch. "Give it to me and help me forget. For a few minutes, help me forget everything!"

Slocum had to abandon his carnal explorations so he could shuck off his gun belt and then work on the buttons holding his fly shut. He sighed in relief when he popped open the last button and let his erection snap out, hard and proud and ready for action. Then it was his turn to gasp in reaction. Antoinette's clever fingers reached around and found the tight little sac dangling beneath his hardened shaft and did a tiny tap dance on it.

Slocum put his hands on the woman's hips to support himself as a wave of delightful weakness flooded through him. Her knowing fingers found all the right spots to touch and move, from the bottom all the way to the arrowheaded tip of his manhood. He stepped closer and rubbed himself against her naked behind, giving them both a hint of more pleasurable activities to come.

"In, hurry, in," she demanded. "There's no need to tease me. I'm ready for you. I am!"

Slocum let her fingers curl around his steely column and draw him forward. The tip touched her nether lips and parted them. He felt the heat boiling from her aroused center, the moistness that betrayed her arousal, the promise of more and better ahead. He stepped a little closer and thrust an inch into her from behind. This small intrusion was enough to cause Antoinette to gasp again and release her grip on him. She had to use both hands to support herself as she leaned forward.

Moving carefully, Slocum inched inward and buried himself full-length in the tightly clinging, womanly tunnel. Hands lightly placed on the woman's hips steadied him but also gave him the chance to pull her back more powerfully into the curve of his groin. This caused him to sink an extra inch into her molten core.

Antoinette began moving her hips now, circling clockwise. Slocum sucked in his breath as the lightning stabs of pure desire blasted into his loins. He began circling in the opposite direction, their counter movements building mutual excitement rapidly.

Then he bent over, his bare chest against her back as he reached around and fumbled with the buttons on her blouse. For an instant Slocum thought he had gone too far. The woman's hand pressed hotly into his, then he realized she was helping him free her lovely breasts. Reaching around when the blouse hung open allowed him to stroke over those firm, proud mounds of succulent flesh. He tried to use both hands, one on each jug, but he couldn't keep his balance that way. He caught one nip between thumb and forefinger and pressed firmly, feeling the flesh pound with blood pumped by her excited heart.

But Slocum finally had to give up and draw his arm around, across her belly so he could hold her in position. Strong inner muscles clamped firmly on him as he stirred about in the tight, damp channel. Feeling his control slipping away, Slocum stopped his rotation and began thrusting, slowly at first and then building speed.

"Oh, oh, yes, that's it. More, oh, oh!"

Slocum could hardly hear the woman's cries of desire. The blood hammered loudly in his ears. He began a deliberate motion in and out, the friction of his manhood against her inner tissues mounting by the instant. He had thought she had aroused him before. Her hand returned between her legs and stroked over the tightness dangling beneath his fleshy shaft.

The carnal heat he generated coupled with the rhythmic squeezing on his balls almost caused him to explode like a volcano. He moved his right arm around a little and began exploring the tangled bush between her thighs. He found the tiny pink spire of flesh at the top of those nether lips and pressed down hard.

The beautiful woman gasped in sudden release. It had all come together for her. The feel of him moving within her, the way her rounded ass pressed into his groin, the touch of his fingers on her most intimate flesh. Antoinette bucked like a bronco, and Slocum rode her for all he was worth.

He held on and tried to keep moving, but her climax contrived to rob him of his control. Heat built deep within, beneath her still stroking fingertips, and then raced along his meaty column to explode outward. His right arm locked around her hips to hold her in place as he spent.

For some time after, he held her like this although he had melted like an icicle in the hot summer sun. Something about simply feeling her close added to his enjoyment, but he finally had to allow her to stand. When she did, she spun in the circle of his arms, stared into his eyes again and then kissed him hard on the lips.

Slocum enjoyed the feel of her naked breasts crushing into his bare chest, her hard nipples rubbing playfully.

Then she stepped back and pulled together her blouse and actually blushed.

"Whatever must you think of me? A fine, proper young woman who lets her animal instincts roam like that!"

"I think highly of you," Slocum said.

"I must tend to you," she said.

"My arm's not aching, hardly at all," Slocum said. But Antoinette dropped to her knees, lightly kissed his flaccid length, then tucked it back into his jeans. It took her almost a minute to rebutton his fly, but Slocum wasn't complaining. The nearness of her face to his crotch, the clever, darting fingers that occasionally touched here and there—her very presence was enough to excite him all over again. But she got to her feet, and pushed down her skirts, then buttoned her blouse and tried vainly to press out the wrinkles.

"That's better," she said.

"Much better," Slocum agreed.

"Now, let's look at that arm. The big one," she said, blushing furiously again.

"My left arm," he said, trying not to laugh.

She took the bottle of antiseptic and carefully cleaned the length of the stitches, then applied a fresh bandage. He winced at the prickling pain.

"You should keep it in a sling for a while longer. The stitches are trying to pull free."

"It's hard to ride with my arm in a sling," Slocum said.

"Stay," she said impulsively. "Stay in Agate. For a while." Antoinette averted her eyes. "I'm sorry. You have business to tend to."

"I have to get your Bible back."

"But you said the robbers took it." She looked at him, eyes wide in surprise. "How can you hope to get it back from them? They're the roughest, toughest band of outlaws south of the Missouri."

"I promised your brother I'd get your legacy to you. I intend to do just that."

"It's important to me," Antoinette said longingly, "but it's nothing to get yourself killed for."

"What's in the Bible that's so precious?"

"The Thibadeaux family history, a genealogy, a few pictures of my ma and pa, another picture of all my siblings. But you can't go after it. You'd be killed. Those are dangerous men and not even the cavalry has been able to catch them—or even find where their hideout is. Pierre told me stories."

"There are always stories," Slocum said. "Thanks for patching me up."

"And thank you," she said coyly, batting her long eyelashes in his direction.

Slocum left the surgery and fumbled in his shirt pocket. He had four dollars that went for necessary supplies, including more ammunition. He felt he'd need it. Then he hit the trail back to the wrecked stagecoach.

He found himself thinking of Antoinette Thibadeaux all the way back.

4

The trail was faint and Slocum relied more on instinct than anything he read on the ground. A day north of the stage-coach wreck he got the uneasy feeling that something was wrong. Dismounting, he let the winded roan drink from a small stream. Slocum studied the ground around him for any spoor from the road agents.

He found horse flop that had cooked in the sun for about the right length of time, but anyone could have come this way. He had no proof he was on any trail, much less the right one. But something else bothered him. Letting the horse graze after drinking its fill, he walked around and climbed to a low rise to study his back trail. He caught his breath when he saw the movement a couple miles where he had just ridden. Another rider had followed him.

Slocum's hand went to the six-shooter holstered at his hip, then fell away. He winced as he stretched his left arm, which had healed rapidly after Antoinette Thibadeaux's expert ministrations. Even the stiffness would be gone in a few more days.

But first he had to deal with the rider behind him. Slocum knew it wasn't a Sioux scout. He would never have spotted a brave. And it wasn't one of Captain Dawson's scouts, not from the way he rode. It might be one of the road agents, forcing Slocum to deal with a backshooter before a bullet found him. Along with the threat, however, came great opportunity, if this was one of the gang that had robbed the stagecoach and killed Zeke. Taken alive, the road agent could be made to tell what happened to the Thibadeaux Bible.

Slocum had learned a great deal about interrogation from the Apache—firsthand.

He considered how best to capture the rider, but it would require some skill on his part. He had stopped to water his horse, and the man on his trail had, too. A mile or two between them didn't offer too much chance for Slocum to get the drop on his persistent shadow.

Squinting, he estimated he had another four hours of sunlight. To the north lay the beginnings of the Black Hills and undoubtedly where the road agents had their hideout. On the prairie he had little chance of sneaking up on his cautious companion, but the foothills afforded a better chance. Slocum returned to his roan and walked it for a mile or so, killing time. Then he mounted and rode toward the low hills he had set his sights on earlier.

By now it was twilight. Slocum wheeled his horse around, cut down a deep ravine and rode for ten minutes before getting back to level ground. He paralleled his original course and then angled in to come up behind the rider, who had picked up the pace to close the distance between them. Slocum suspected he would have been murdered in his bedroll sometime during the night if he hadn't been alert.

He dismounted and waited as night fell and the bright spray of stars above provided the only illumination. Slocum was in no hurry, but he waited so long for the rider that he thought the man might have turned away and headed in some other direction. Slocum vowed to wait another half hour—patience had always been a virtue with him. A slow smile crossed his lips when he heard the soft *clop-clop* of a horse's hooves after another twenty minutes.

Slocum crouched and let the dry grass brush against his shoulders. He heard his roan making small noises some distance behind him but doubted the sound would carry far enough to alert the rider. His hand resting on the butt of his pistol, Slocum waited for the rider to appear. Even with the bright starlight he couldn't make out the man's face because of the way the hat brim was pulled down low. All he saw was a vague silhouette, but the horse and rider came directly for him. Slocum didn't move a muscle until the rider was even with him.

Legs like springs, Slocum shot up, grabbed at the rider's arm and dragged him from the saddle.

"Don't move," Slocum said, whipping out his six-shooter in a smooth action. "You're going to tell me everything I want to know or I'll drill you."

"Is that a promise, John?"

Slocum stood with his six-gun pointed at the supine figure. He recognized the voice instantly.

"Antoinette!"

"Who else would follow you for so long?"

"It's been two days. You trailed me from Agate?"

"There was nothing to keep me there." For a moment, the dark figure stirred, then held out a hand. "Are you going to help me up or are you going to join me down here?"

He holstered his six-shooter and grabbed Antoinette's hand to pull her to her feet.

"You shouldn't have come. If I find those outlaws, it'll get dangerous mighty fast." He remembered the sight of Zeke Maharis stretched out on the prairie, the coyotes half done with their feeding by the time Slocum arrived. The road agents had left the dead man behind because they didn't give a good goddamn.

When he caught up with the stagecoach driver's murderers, it was going to get really bloody—it would be no place for a woman.

"I can take care of myself. Not as good as you with a

pistol, but I'm a decent shot with a rifle or shotgun. Want to see?"

"No," Slocum said. "I ought to put you across my lap and paddle you before sending you back to Agate."

"Promises, promises," Antoinette teased. Then her tone turned more somber. "I have to help, John. You said the Sioux killed Pierre, but the men who stole our Bible are responsible, too. They caused the patrols out of Fort Robinson to be split. You said Pierre had only a squad with him. For such a mission, there ought to have been twice that number."

Slocum wasn't going to debate the finer points of how a cavalry troop worked. She might be right, but he thought Pete and his squad would have still ridden alone, outlaws or not.

"Let's make a camp and discuss what to do," Slocum said. Antoinette moved closer to him and put her arm around him for support. She hobbled a little as they retrieved her horse and went to fetch Slocum's roan.

"Did I hurt you when I pulled you off your horse?"

"It's nothing. Feels about like a pebble in my shoe. It won't hold me back. I won't get in your way."

"You're already in my way," Slocum said. "I need to concentrate completely on trailing. It's been hard, since the trail is cold, and the outlaws rode so fast that they didn't leave much sign behind them."

"Then my eyes will help by looking where yours aren't," Antoinette said. "You look for the trail, I'll keep a sharp lookout for the highwaymen themselves. This is their country, after all."

"That's what worries me," Slocum said. He built a small fire, banked it and boiled some water from a creek for coffee. The smell would carry for miles if a night breeze caught the aroma, but at the moment it was deathly still.

"I've endured a lot worse than outlaws, John," Antoinette said.

"Of course you have," he said. "You were a school teacher in Agate."   •

She laughed at his joke, then said, "I dealt with some hard cases in that schoolhouse, that's for sure. But doctoring the town was worse. I've never seen such a lot of crybabies, all coming to me with the teeniest of ailments."

It was Slocum's turn to laugh. The lovely woman truly had no idea why the men of Agate developed so many aches, pains and maladies. With women scarce on the prairie, what man wouldn't want Antoinette Thibadeaux fussing over him, at least for a few minutes?

"What happened to the town's doctor?"

"He upped and disappeared one day. That's not too unusual around Agate, from what I hear. The blacksmith disappeared, as well. One day he was hammering out horseshoes, the next he was gone. I doubt the doctor felt much appreciated by the townspeople so he moved on but the blacksmith had a good business. Agate is a farming town and Bill Benbow was an expert at fixing plowshares. No matter how nicked or busted up it was, he could fix it. Saved more than one farmer a fortune having to buy new iron and steel implements."

Slocum listened with half an ear. Residents of western towns came and went like dust motes in a strong wind.

"Doctor Zacharias left his ledger behind. Everyone owed him money. One of them might have shot him and left him out on the prairie rather than pay."

"Had he lost any patients? Sometimes a man's ire is raised if he thinks a sawbones let a loved one die."

"Doc Zacharias lost patients all the time, but from what I could tell, nobody blamed him much. No, the ones who survived simply didn't pay him." Antoinette laughed musically. "They always paid me."

Slocum found that quite believable. He stared at the gorgeous woman, her face turned elfin by the dancing shadows cast by the cooking fire.

"Why'd you come to Nebraska?" he asked. She looked as if she'd be more at home in some elegant New Orleans parlor, dressed up in a fancy ball gown and exchanging clever witticisms with other high society ladies.

"Pete joined the Army and was stationed at Fort Robinson. I followed along, but there wasn't anything for me to do at the post, so I found Agate and fit in there. For a while. I was beginning to get tired of the town."

"Too small?"

"Something like that. No excitement."

Slocum reckoned this might be the heart of the matter. Antoinette needed stimulation and wasn't likely to get it in a sleepy town like Agate. That it took Slocum coming to tell her about her brother's death and the stolen family Bible to give her a little thrill was a shame.

"You'll have to go back. If I find the road agents, it'll get mighty exciting. Too exciting, too dangerous. You're going to have to go back to Agate and wait."

"Is it dangerous right now? Maybe I'd better get a little closer so you can . . . protect . . . me."

Antoinette moved her bedroll beside Slocum's, and he did his best to protect her. With the woman in his arms later, he began drifting off to sleep, only to jerk fully awake at a distant sound.

"Wha' sit?" Antoinette murmured sleepily.

"A stagecoach," Slocum said. "Odd time for one to be on the road." He tried to figure out what time it was and decided it was at least another hour until dawn.

"Won't go back to Agate. Like it here," Antoinette said, clinging to him and then going back to sleep.

The rumble of the stage wheels receded, making him wonder if he had ever heard it. By the time he woke again, it was to the smell of frying bacon. Antoinette fussed about the fire, poking at the bacon with a green twig she had picked up. Coffee already boiled in a pot.

"Smells good," Slocum said. He stretched and was pleased that his left arm gave only a slight twinge. He was about healed from the Sioux knife thrust.

"I'm not that good a cook, not on the trail. In a kitchen I can whup up a pretty fair meal."

"Did you hear a stagecoach last night?" Slocum asked suddenly. The matter took on importance beyond a half-remembered dream, for some reason.

"Why, yes, I did. It was close-by, too."

Slocum ate his breakfast in silence, thinking hard. When they had packed their gear he made only a nominal attempt to chase Antoinette back to Agate. He realized shooing her away would be like swatting at a determined fly. The more he protested, the more she would bedevil him. For the moment it was better to keep an eye on her. When he had a more definite plan, he would make certain she was safely away from the danger.

"Where to?" she asked.

"The stagecoach bothers me. Why was it traveling at night?"

"It might have been in a real hurry," she said, "but I don't remember any stage line ever being that determined to keep to schedule. The drivers prefer to get liquored up at some way station rather than driving at night."

They rode in silence for two miles until Slocum came across the tracks. The stagecoach had cut directly across the prairie, shunning the road visible through the low grass.

"Heading north," he said, more to himself than to Antoinette. Louder, he asked, "What's the nearest town?"

"Parson's Grove is that way," Antoinette said, squinting as she got her bearings, staring into the rising sun. "How far, I don't know. Maybe five miles. Ten?"

Slocum never hesitated. He turned his roan toward Parson's Grove and eventually crossed the road, which they followed all day into the town, arriving almost at sundown. In some ways Parson's Grove was indistinguishable from Agate, but Slocum felt a tension here that was lacking in the other Nebraska prairie town. People peered at them as they rode down the main street, only to dart away if Slocum turned toward them. Curtains fluttered and made him suspect even more townspeople watched surreptitiously.

"I can use some real food," Antoinette said. "There's a nice looking restaurant."

"The only one," Slocum replied. "I'll stable the horses and have them looked after. Go on into the restaurant and wait."

Antoinette hesitated, then nodded brusquely. She obviously wondered if he would try to strand her, then had decided he wouldn't. He had said he would meet her in the restaurant. Slocum was glad she recognized that his word was his bond. Too many men these days lied too easily, when it suited their purposes.

He led the horses down the street to the livery stables and had to shout for someone to come out. A young man, hardly out of his teens, fearfully looked around the side of the barn.

"What you wantin'?"

"Grain for the horses, someone to curry and water them. To take care of them," Slocum said, wondering if the young man was a bit dense. "Why else would I bring horses to a livery?"

"Never kin tell," the youth said, edging around. "I ain't the owner. Don't know where he got off to. I been runnin' the place 'til he gets back."

Slocum read more into the words. The young man had implied, "if he gets back."

"A lot of folks just take off and never come back?" Slocum wasn't sure why he asked, but from the way the young man jumped, he knew he had hit a bull's-eye. He just didn't know what it implied about Parson's Grove.

"Two bits. For each horse," the stableman said.

Slocum paid him and returned to the restaurant. It was deserted other than for Antoinette sitting at a table near the large plate glass window.

"Folks in these parts are mighty jumpy," Slocum said as he sat. "Sounds like they might be disappearing."

"Disappearing? You mean they just pull up stakes and move on? Is that so unusual?"

"The stable owner left and never bothered telling anyone. What looks to be his only employee is keeping things going, but he's not doing that good a job."

"Curious," Antoinette said. She looked up and smiled brightly when a man in a stained apron came over. "I'm famished. What is your specialty?"

The waiter swallowed hard, then shook his head. "Not got much but stew. No business lately."

"Everyone leaving on the stagecoach?" Slocum asked. He got the same reaction from the waiter he had from the stableman. The waiter's eyes went wide as he took a half step backward.

"Why'd you say that?"

"Heard the stage rumbling across the prairie this morning before sunup," Slocum said.

"Stage was . . . robbed."

"Robbed?" Slocum knew there had to be more to the story. "What do you mean?"

"They took everything. The team, the coach, driver, all the passengers, anything being carried."

"They?" asked Antoinette lightly, but Slocum saw the tension come to her face. "Who might 'they' be?"

"The outlaws. Nobody's safe from them." The waiter looked around the otherwise empty dining room, as if he were betraying some confidence.

"What's the law doing about them?" asked Slocum.

"The law cain't do nuthin'. Fact is, the marshal hightailed it sometime last week. We don't even have any lawman in town now."

"Then you should rely on the cavalry over at Fort Robinson," Antoinette said. "Send a message to the commanding officer and ask for a detachment to be stationed here until you find another marshal."

"They don't know nuthin' neither," the waiter said uneasily. "They're denyin' there's any trouble. Now do you want the stew? That's all we got."

"Stew," Slocum said, "for two."

The waiter hurried off, leaving them to stare out into the main street of Parson's Grove, each lost in thought. Twilight deepened into night by the time the waiter returned with their dinner.

"No lights," Slocum observed as he spooned the tepid stew into his mouth. "There aren't any lights anywhere up and down the street."

"You're right. Not even at the saloon. That is a saloon across the street, isn't it?"

Slocum nodded. The windows were closed and the citizens of Parson's Grove went to ground like frightened prairie dogs. He and Antoinette finished their dinner and went outside onto the boardwalk and strolled up and down the street, taking in the sights.

"There's only one hotel, John," she said. "We should get rooms."

"Before everyone else beats us to them?" Slocum said sarcastically. He had ridden through ghost towns that were more lively than Parson's Grove.

"Before I fall over from exhaustion," Antoinette said. "You did keep me up a considerable part of the night last night."

"You kept a considerable part of me up last night, too," Slocum said, steering her toward the three-story brick hotel next to the town bakery. A light shone from the side door in the bakery and mouthwatering smells drifted out. The rest of Parson's Grove was hiding but the baker toiled away at his work.

"Should we conserve?" she asked.

Slocum stared at her.

Antoinette grinned and explained, "Why spend money for two rooms when one with a large enough bed will suffice?"

"The clerk might talk." Slocum worried about her reputation. If such a sleeping arrangement became public knowledge, she would never get another job teaching school. From the twinkle in her eye, Slocum saw this was the least of Antoinette's worries at the moment.

"We'll conserve our meager funds," she said decisively.

They registered, the clerk eying them fearfully.

"Is there anything wrong?" Antoinette asked sweetly.

"You folks do anything special?" the clerk asked.

"I don't follow you," Slocum said before Antoinette could answer. "What do you mean?"

"Any special trade? Skills?"

"Why, I can do a bit of doctoring," Antoinette said. "Does someone need a doctor?"

Slocum wondered at the clerk's reaction. The man turned three shades paler as he shook his head. Without another word, he passed over a key to the room at the head of the stairs on the second floor. Slocum took the key and followed Antoinette to the room. The instant he opened the door, he had to smile.

"The bakery's right under our window. That's a nice change from the usual smells in a town."

"So it is," Antoinette said, pushing up the curtain and opening the window fully. She sucked in a deep breath, then looked at Slocum. "What are you staring at?"

"Take another deep breath," he said.

"Oh, men!" She reached over and threw a pillow at him, but they ended up on the bed wrestling delightfully.

As they drifted off to sleep, Slocum heard horses approaching, then voices below them at the bakery. Disengaging his arm from around Antoinette, he got to his feet and peered out the window.

Three men wearing long, dark dusters, hats pulled low on their foreheads, entered the side door. From inside the bakery came a single loud shout, followed by silence. Immediately the three men left, two of them supporting a fourth between them. The third man brought around horses. The fourth man was draped belly down over a saddle. The other three mounted and rode slowly from town.

Slocum considered riding after them, but his horse was stabled across town, and the roan's wind had been broken. It wasn't up to traveling all day and then doing it again all night. Antoinette stirred on the bed, her arm flailing about as she hunted for him. Slocum returned to bed, snuggling close behind the woman, their bodies fitting together like spoons in a drawer.

There'd be time in the morning to find out an explanation for what he'd just witnessed.

5

Slocum was up early the next morning and went to the window. The fragrant aroma of baking bread was gone. Only an acrid stench rose from the bakery below the window. Slocum thought this came from loaves of bread left in the oven to burn to a cinder. He dressed quietly, strapped on his gun belt and settled the Colt Navy at his hip, then slipped from the room without waking Antoinette.

The clerk had curled up behind the counter and still snored noisily. Passing without waking the clerk proved easy for Slocum. He stepped into the humid, still predawn and looked around. Most farming towns were up and about before sunrise. Not Parson's Grove. The people still huddled behind their closed shutters and curtained windows. Slocum turned and went to the side door of the bakery and poked his head inside, not sure what he'd find. The burned smell came stronger. He went to the oven, opened the door and saw the charred remains of a dozen bread loaves. Using tongs hanging beside the oven, he pulled the tray out and dumped the contents on the floor before closing the door. The wood oven had not been stoked or fed all night, but the heat still made the room almost unbearable.

Walking slowly through the shop, Slocum looked at everything he could, trying to piece together what had happened the night before. The scene began to build until he got a hard lump in the pit of his stomach. The baker had been kidnapped. That was the only conclusion he could reach, remembering what he had seen and adding to it evidence in the bakery. Flour bins had been knocked over and a new batch of bread had been kneaded and left to rise but had been untouched since. That, with the burned loaves in the oven, told Slocum the baker had not left willingly.

He stepped back into the street where the first light of dawn sparked some life in Parson's Grove. He made a bee-line to the marshal's office, but it was as the waiter had told them the night before. Dust had settled on the lawman's desk and the cell doors stood ajar. Slocum couldn't even find the keys to open the doors. The rifles and shotguns usually racked in a marshal's office were gone, as was all the ammunition from drawers below the empty racks. Again Slocum poked through the office, hunting for something to tell him what was going on in town.

The missing rifles weren't odd, but the lack of wanted posters was. Anyone coming into an abandoned office was likely to help himself to the weapons, but why take the wanted posters? They were scraps of paper and nothing more without a marshal to arrest and enforce the law.

Crossing the street to the saloon, Slocum rapped loudly on the locked front door. He heard grumbling inside and the double doors opened a crack. A bloodshot eye peered at him.

"What do you want?"

"A drink," Slocum said.

"It's too early."

"It was already too late when I got into town last evening," Slocum said. "There an ordinance against serving liquor in Parson's Grove?"

"No," the man said reluctantly. He poked a shaggy head out and looked up and down the street before asking, "Just you?"

"I've got enough thirst for two men," Slocum said. When he saw the reaction, he added, "Just me."

"Come on in and be quick about it." The barkeep went behind the bar and stopped a moment, his hands lingering under the stained wood. Slocum saw the reflection in the long mirror behind the bar. The bartender gripped a sawed-off shotgun with all the determination of a man clinging to life.

"A beer." Slocum dropped a nickel on the bar, letting it ring musically. The lure of money loosened the barkeep's grip. He picked up a dirty mug and drew a frothy-headed beer for Slocum.

Slocum wanted to shout "Boo!" and watch the reaction, but he didn't want buckshot flying around. The barkeep's hand had returned to the handle of the shotgun the instant he had served the beer.

"Town's mighty quiet," Slocum said. "Even the bakery's quiet, especially after the ruckus there last night."

"What ruckus might that be?"

"When the three men dragged the baker out."

"Never happened," the barkeep said nervously. Sweat beaded on the man's bald head and his long mustache quivered in reaction.

"Why's that?"

"Ain't no baker in Parson's Grove. Never has been."

"Why have a bakery if there's no baker? Seems someone was mighty intent on baking bread last night."

"Get out of here. We don't want your kind in Parson's Grove."

"What kind might that be?" asked Slocum, not hurrying as he sipped at the beer.

"The kind who ask too damn many questions!" The barkeep grabbed for the shotgun but Slocum was already moving. He left a trail of beer and foam as he swung the mug at the side of the man's head. There was a dull crunch as glass met bone and knocked the bartender flat on the floor. His limp fingers still curled around the shotgun, but Slocum saw the man wasn't going to make any further trouble. Slocum tossed the mug aside, reached over the bar and grabbed a bottle of whiskey and took a quick pull. The heat all the way down to his belly finally woke him up and chased away the cobwebs in his brain.

He had been cut and shot at and presented with too many mysteries and the whiskey helped. A lot.

Wiping his lips, Slocum left the saloon and saw Parson's Grove had developed a semblance of life during his brief sojourn at the saloon. He glanced in the direction of the bakery. People walking past pointedly averted their eyes away from the building, as if denying it even existed. Slocum wondered what other businesses in town were similarly treated—and similarly forcibly abandoned.

Slocum walked quickly to the restaurant and went in. The waiter looked up from a table where he was eating breakfast.

"Ain't open yet," the waiter said.

Slocum crossed the room and grabbed a handful of throat. His strong fingers squeezed until the waiter turned fiery red in the face as he gasped for breath.

"I'll ask once. Where does the town baker live? The man who ran the bakery? Where?" Slocum shook like a terrier with a rat between his jaws.

As he loosened his grip, the waiter panted harshly.

"Outside of town. Mile or so east of here. Whitewashed picket fence around it. Only one."

Slocum spun and left, going directly to the stables. The young man who ran it in place of the actual owner was nowhere to be seen. Slocum saddled his and Antoinette's horses and led them into the street, lashing them to the hitching post beside the hotel. As he went into the lobby, Antoinette was coming down the stairs.

"Let's take a small ride," Slocum said.

"Where, John?"

He glanced toward the desk and saw the top of a head

dip back down out of sight. She saw his quick look and nodded, hurrying to leave the hotel lobby and the eaves-dropping clerk.

Outside, Slocum explained what had happened.

"I thought I was dreaming," Antoinette said. "You getting up and going to the window, the sounds, the smell of baking bread changing to a burned smell. What do you make of it?"

"The baker was kidnapped and nobody in town will admit it. I don't know why." He swung into the saddle and waited for Antoinette to mount.

"I see what you mean," Antoinette said, watching as two men hurried in front of the bakery, eyes pointedly turned from the store. "What does it mean?"

"Might be there'll be answers at the baker's house. The waiter at the restaurant was kind enough to give me the information when the barkeep denied there ever being a baker in town."

"Now why do I get the feeling he wasn't speaking freely?"

"He told me everything I wanted to know of his own accord." Slocum flexed his hand, remembering the feel of the waiter's throat beneath his fingers.

They rode in silence and eventually Slocum spotted the white picket fence around a small, neatly kept house.

"That must be the place. Only one with a fence, just as the waiter said."

"We ought to be careful, John. If the baker had enemies who took him away and killed him, they might be lurking, waiting for his friends to come out."

"From the way everyone in Parson's Grove acts, nobody will own up to being a friend of anyone else." Slocum still took Antoinette's advice and slipped the leather thong off the hammer of his six-shooter and made sure it slid easily in the holster. They rode closer and then drew rein, watching and waiting.

No children laughing and playing. No adults doing chores. A few chickens out back clucked and squawked, but Slocum didn't even see a dog.

"Wait here. I'll be right back."

"Wait? Wait?" protested Antoinette. "I'm going with you. This place gives me the willies."

"It's too quiet," Slocum said.

"As quiet as a grave."

Slocum walked up the flagstone path to the front door. It stood ajar. He pushed it open with the toe of his boot, drew his six-gun and went into the house. He didn't know what to make of what he saw.

"It's empty. All the furniture is gone, the pictures are off the walls, everything's gone!" exclaimed Antoinette.

Slocum saw the discolored sections on the walls where pictures had protected the paint underneath. Once removed, the darker sections took on the appearance of pictures. Phantom pictures. He moved quickly through the house. Every stick of furniture, every stitch of clothing, everything had been taken.

"You were right about there being a dog, John," called Antoinette from out back. "There's a pile of bones, all chewed like a dog would do."

Slocum joined her, thinking some wild creatures might have devoured the residents of the house, but Antoinette was right. He identified a couple beef bones that would have been given to a faithful dog. A quick check showed the barn was similarly empty, though much of the equipment remained. But the entire area looked as if the baker and his family—a wife and possibly two children, with their dog—had simply packed everything and left.

If he hadn't seen how the baker was dragged from his bakery, Slocum would have thought the man had simply left Parson's Grove to find a better life elsewhere.

"How many others?" he wondered aloud. Antoinette Thibadeaux stared at him. "How many others from Parson's Grove have simply disappeared one night?"

"The marshal?"

"The marshal, the livery stable owner, the baker. How many others? The stagecoach, driver and every passenger in it? And why?"

Slocum found it much easier to ask the questions than to answer them.

6

They rode back to Parson's Grove, each lost in their own thoughts. Slocum had seen the baker being kidnapped, and the recent removal of everything from the man's house—including his family and their dog—screamed that something was seriously wrong. Slocum had seen blood feuds that included an entire family, but never had he seen the people and their belongings all taken in this manner. If someone had such a powerful hatred toward the baker, why not burn down the house, too?

And Slocum kept coming back to one undeniable fact. Even the dog was missing.

"I can find the tracks back at the house," Slocum said suddenly. He had worked it through and knew that, as important as retrieving the stolen Bible might be to Antoinette, he had to find the baker and do what he could for the man's family. He didn't even know the baker's name, but that didn't matter. Something was seriously wrong, and it rankled Slocum that he couldn't figure out what it was.

"We'll need some supplies from the store in town," Antoinette said.

"No." Slocum spat out the word. "Where I'm going, you couldn't keep up. Even if you could, I don't want to spend all my time looking over my shoulder, worrying about your safety. That'd get us both killed."

"I'm not giving up, John," she said firmly. "You know me well enough by now to know that I am not a quitter."

"There's more going on around here than road agents holding up stagecoaches," Slocum said. "People are disappearing, and nobody'll face up to it."

"You think the town marshal was kidnapped, too?"

"Maybe not him, but the livery stable owner might have vanished the same way the baker did. If the stableman left in charge hadn't been so obviously scared out of his skin, I'd think he had done away with the owner so he could take over a thriving business without having to buy it." Slocum shook his head. "The man at the stable looks frightened, as if he might be next to disappear."

"If you won't let me go with you, and you can spot me if I trail you, what am I supposed to do? I don't have much money, and I'll be damned if I will return to Agate."

"The town might be missing a few essential professions. Look around and see if you can't set yourself up as doctor or schoolmarm or something else in Parson's Grove. It won't be for long, and I'm sure you can do about anything—for a while."

"I thought so, too," Antoinette said, "until I tried to bend my legs into that position you wanted last night. I swear, I almost broke my back!"

Slocum had to laugh. Antoinette knew when to lighten the mood. He sobered and went on.

"Do something that will bring you in touch with as many of the townspeople as possible, listen to them, talk to them, find out what's going on. They know. I'm sure they do, but they are afraid of outsiders. That tells me whatever's bedeviling them isn't caused by anyone already in town." He eyed the towering Black Hills to the north. That was the way the trail he had followed earlier was leading. He suspected the trail from the baker's house would lead in the same direction.

"What of the stagecoach? The one you heard in the night? Is that part of the mystery?" asked Antoinette.

"Could be. It doesn't make any more sense than anything else we've come across."

"I suppose Parson's Grove has a doctor already. I might get a job as a nurse. Or a clerk in the general store. Everyone comes through a store eventually to buy supplies and sit around the pickle barrel." Antoinette turned toward him, her blue eyes tinkling. "Or if I sweet-talked the owner, I could get a job as a hurdy-gurdy girl at the saloon."

"You'd certainly liven up the town," Slocum said, refusing to rise to the bait.

Antoinette laughed when she saw she was not going to make him the least bit jealous.

"No need for you to ride back with me to town," she said, "not if the real trail to follow is back at the house. Go on, John. I'll be fine."

Slocum nodded and started to turn his roan's face when she reached out and grabbed the bridle, causing the horse to turn back. Antoinette tugged a bit and came alongside Slocum and gave him a big kiss.

"Don't think you can sneak off like that, not without a kiss for good luck."

"That one was off-center," Slocum said. "Maybe you should do it again."

"Oh, you!" She reached back and gave his horse's rump a sharp swat. The roan was so tired it hardly responded but it did carry Slocum a few feet past her. "Don't you get into so much trouble I can't patch you up again," she warned. The words carried more than a little concern for him, though.

Slocum wasted no time trotting back to the deserted house. He tried to put Antoinette Thibadeaux from his mind, but it was hard. She was a resourceful, clever woman and could look after herself. Still, Slocum had no idea what they were up against. It defied explanation right now because he didn't have enough facts. But the best way of finding out those answers was to be sure Antoinette was in town, surrounded by others who might help out if the going got rough.

From all he had seen, that help might not be forthcoming, not if the citizens of Parson's Grove refused to even admit there had been a baker with loaves of bread baking in the oven when he had been kidnapped. And the man's entire family had been spirited away, too. Where were their friends?

Slocum rode around the house, just outside the picket fence, studying the ground. He found evidence of several horses behind the house—and something that completely perplexed him. Dismounting, Slocum dropped to his hands and knees and studied the tracks. He measured them with the span of his hand, then stood and paced off the distance between the wheel marks.

"I'll be damned," he muttered. "They drove a stage-coach away from the house." The best he could figure, whoever had taken the baker and his family had pulled up in a stagecoach, probably loaded it with belongings from the house and then driven off. Slocum started walking, parallel with the tracks and saw how they deepened, confirming that the stagecoach was lighter when it arrived than when it departed. He could almost picture the family dog sitting atop the stage, barking as they vanished in a cloud of dust.

Slocum shook off the mental image and got his horse, this time following the trail from the saddle. The roan stumbled often, and Slocum knew he should have traded mounts with Antoinette. The last thing he wanted was for the strawberry roan to die under him when he needed to make a speedy retreat.

By sundown Slocum had reached the foothills of the Black Range and discovered it almost impossible to follow even a heavily laden stagecoach. The ground had turned to stone and refused to yield up more than a scrape or a scratch. By the time the sun set, Slocum had to admit he had lost the trail amid winding canyon trails leading back into the Black Hills.

It had been a long day, and Slocum vowed to find the tracks in the morning, after he'd had a good night's sleep. The prior night had been more arousing than relaxing for him, Antoinette keeping him busy most of the time he should have been sleeping. He stretched his left arm and felt only a slight tug where she had tended the stitches. As far as he was concerned, he was back to fighting strength, but he couldn't say the same for his horse. The animal had turned listless late in the day and stumbled often. Once its wind had been broken by the hard riding he had done, he doubted it would ever be the same.

As he fixed himself a cold meal, not knowing how far ahead the men who had kidnapped the baker and his entire family might be, he took a deep whiff of the humid night air and caught the scent of roasting meat.

"Venison," he said softly, staring at the slab of jerky he had gnawed down to a nubbin. His mouth watered as more of the savory smell reached him. Slocum stashed his jerky and went exploring, hand resting on the butt of his Colt as he went.

He saw the Indian sentry before being spotted. Dropping flat, Slocum inched forward and got past the brave. Closer to the camp he saw a half dozen Indians laughing and jostling one another playfully, all the while eating freshly cooked venison. Slocum studied them to see if there was any chance he might steal some of their bountiful meal, then realized he wasn't spying on a Sioux camp. These were Blackfoot.

Edging back, he passed the sentry again and then stood. He took a deep breath and advanced on the brave, his hands held out to the sides of his body so that, even in the dark, it was obvious he did not bear a weapon.

"I would speak with the chief of the mighty Blackfoot,"

Slocum called to the sentry. The brave whirled about, rifle levelled. Slocum held his breath, hoping the guard wouldn't simply put a bullet in him. He had done all he could so the Indian would save face. No one need ever know had spied on them after sneaking past the sentry.

"Who you?"

"My name's Slocum, and I come with a gift for your chief."

"Gift?"

"For your chief," Slocum repeated firmly. This might have sparked a demand for a gift to be given to the sentry, but the others in the camp had heard the loud exchange and came to investigate. Slocum immediately turned to the tall, rangy brave he had pegged as their leader. He gave his spiel about being a traveller with gifts to trade with the famous Blackfoot leader and only hoped he found out the hunter's name before it became obvious he was only taking a stab in the dark.

"I am Dark Cloud," the leader of the hunting party said proudly.

"A mighty chief and a great hunter," Slocum said. "I bring a gift for you."

"Come," the Blackfoot said, obviously intrigued at the prospect of getting anything from a white eyes in such a strange fashion. Slocum heaved a sigh of relief. The stories he had heard about the Blackfoot being peaceful—for the moment—were true.

They sat cross-legged around the cooking fire, taking each other's measure. Slocum finally reached into his pocket and took out the fixings he had for his cigarettes. Back in Agate he had gotten a new pouch of tobacco but had not had the time to smoke any of it. He was glad now that it was intact. He showed it to Dark Cloud, letting the firelight dance on the shiny silver foil before handing it over.

"For your great councils. May your decisions always be wise, Dark Cloud."

The Indian took the tobacco pouch solemnly and opened it with a quick rip. As if by magic, a pipe appeared and the others in the hunting party gathered close, seeking their own places around the fire. This told Slocum Dark Cloud wasn't too high in the hierarchy of the Blackfoot. If anything, this might be the young warrior's first time leading a hunting party.

Slocum sat silently as Dark Cloud crammed a wad of tobacco into the pipe, lit it and inhaled deeply before passing it to the next hunter. The pipe made its way around the circle until it came to Slocum, who joined the ceremony, puffed and passed it to the Indian on his right.

"We smoke in peace," Dark Cloud said. Slocum echoed the sentiment.

Then Slocum asked, "Do you see other white men in this, your land? I seek them because they have stolen something of mine." Telling the Indians he sought a Bible—and white men kidnapped by other white men— would produce no results.

"You are not like the other white eyes," Dark Cloud said after a respectful time. "You are not afraid of those who live in the mountains."

"Why should I be?"

"They raid your villages and take captives. Many captives." A touch of envy came to the Blackfoot's tone now. He obviously remembered the days of raiding and fighting with great longing.

"Where do they go?"

"There. Beyond the hills. We do not go there. They have many guns. Many, many guns."

"I seek those in a stagecoach." Slocum saw from their response that Dark Cloud and the braves with him had seen the stage rumbling through their land.

"We do not follow. We hunt."

"You are a great hunter. That is good venison." Slocum's belly grumbled, so he rubbed it and pointed at the sizzling meat. Dark Cloud motioned for him to eat.

Slocum did so without showing how famished he was. The Indians left something to be desired as cooks, but he hardly noticed that some of the meat was raw while other portions were charred. It went down a considerable bit easier than the maggot-infested jerky he had been eating.

More tobacco was smoked while Slocum finished his portion of the meat. He licked his fingers clean and felt more alert than before he had eaten.

"Do these men attack the Blackfoot?" he asked.

"No! We do not permit it. They raid only their own kind. Your kind."

Slocum found this interesting. The Indians and the outlaws kept their distance, neither bothering the other. It was a good arrangement, more for the road agents than the Blackfoot, but both benefitted. The outlaws had a secure hideout, and the Blackfoot weren't likely to be bothered as they roved through the Black Hills populated by their enemies, the Sioux.

"You are wise to avoid them, since they are bad men," Slocum said. He skirted the matter of having Dark Cloud pinpoint where the outlaw hideout might be. The more Slocum heard, the more curious he got. Stagecoaches being stolen, bakers and stable owners kidnapped, entire towns terrorized—why? He had no answer. But he would.

By the time the tobacco was all smoked, Slocum was itching to be on his way, but the Blackfoot leader surprised him.

"You give Dark Cloud gift. You get gift." The Indian gestured, then spoke rapidly in his own tongue. There was some argument among the other hunters, verifying Slocum's guess that Dark Cloud was on his first hunt as leader. But he had the makings of a real chief and convinced the others to do his bidding.

A smallish horse was led out.

"Gift from Dark Cloud."

"I am grateful to have such a powerful and generous friend," Slocum said. Indians considered their horses to be more valuable than any white man valued gold. Although this horse was small and probably ill-suited to hunting or raiding, giving it to Slocum showed a willingness to become true friends. Moreover, Slocum guessed that it cemented Dark Cloud's leadership over the others.

"May all your hunts be successful."

"Death to your enemies," Dark Cloud answered.

Slocum took the hackamore and steadied the horse, then jumped onto it. The horse shied a little at the weight but quickly calmed. Slocum touched the brim of his hat and rode slowly from the Blackfoot camp, marvelling at his good luck. For a pouch of tobacco he had gained a second horse—and valuable information.

7

The town was smaller than most Slocum had seen in north-western Nebraska. The main street stretched less than twenty yards, accommodating a saloon, a general store, a couple empty stores and a jailhouse. Slocum looked around for a sign telling him the town's name but couldn't find it. That hardly mattered since some towns came and wont oo fast that it never occurred to anyone to put a name to where the most folks lived. Towns like that suited Slocum more than the ones with mayors and city councils and concerned citizens and laws so obscure that even a lawyer got a headache thinking about enforcing them all.

He tethered both his horses in front of the saloon and stretched tired muscles. He had taken to riding the pony given him by Dark Cloud to rest the roan, but the broken-down horse never seemed to recover its strength. Slocum thought seriously of selling it for what he could, if anyone was dumb enough to buy such a worthless animal. The Indian pony, small though it was, proved far more durable. Slocum wondered at Dark Cloud giving it to him and decided it had to do with tribal politics. Dark Cloud had probably given the horse to him rather than to another brave, to put that brave in his place and cement his own leadership. The horse wasn't the big, strapping animal a chief would ride, so Dark Cloud had no reason to keep it in his own remuda. If there was some other reason for the Blackfoot's generosity, Slocum didn't much care. He had traded a pouch of tobacco for a horse. That amounted to a good day's swapping, no matter what.

Walking slowly into the saloon, he looked around. The inside was shabby, befitting a town with a couple dozen inhabitants. Two bottles of whiskey resided on the back bar alongside a beer tap. Slocum looked around to see if a lunch had been put out for customers but saw nothing edible on the bar or any of the tables.

"Howdy, mister, come on in and wet your whistle," called the barkeep. The man was small, wiry and his eyes darted around like a cornered rat, in spite of his warm greeting. He wiped his grimy hands on an equally filthy apron as he went behind the bar and leaned forward, waiting for Slocum's order.

"A beer," Slocum decided. A shot of the whiskey might set well, but he had damned little money left. He needed to find a job for a week or so to earn enough to keep hunting for the men who had stolen Antoinette's Bible. But in his gut he knew finding the Bible as quickly as possible was coupled with the disappearance of the baker and his family. And probably the disappearance of others, too.

"We're kinda outta the way around here," the barkeep said. "You just passin' through?"

"On my way to Parson's Grove," Slocum said.

"What's there?"

Slocum shrugged and sipped the beer. It was so bitter he almost spat it out.

"Not too good, is it? We had a fine brewer right here in town but—" The bartender cut off the words as if they burned his tongue.

"But he just vanished?" Slocum saw the barkeep turn pale.

"Didn't say that. Don't know where he upped and went. Somewhere else."

"Like most of the citizens of this fine town?" asked Slocum.

"Don't know what you mean."

"Most of the stores are empty. This is a dying town."

"Ain't unusual. Happens all the time, everywhere."

Slocum nodded at that. The barkeep was right, but his reaction to questions about the brewer who had once whipped up a better beer was peculiar. Slocum guessed that the brewer, like the baker in Parson's Grove, had turned up missing one morning, all his equipment—and maybe his family, if he had any—gone, too.

He finished the beer and left without another word. The barkeep glared at him all the way out into the street. Slocum turned toward the jailhouse and went to it, knocked and went in. He had expected the office to be deserted as the one in Parson's Grove was, but a bulky man with a big, bushy salt-and-pepper beard sat behind the desk. As the man turned he showed a sheriff's badge.

"What kin I do fer you, mister?" the sheriff asked.

"I wondered if there was a report of a missing stagecoach," Slocum said. "I thought I heard one rumbling along a few nights ago while I was camped out on the prairie."

"We're a ways from the flatlands. Black Hills start around here," the sheriff said.

Slocum waited, saying nothing more. He had asked a straightforward question and had gotten a geography lesson.

"What brings you to this little town?" the sheriff asked.

"A missing stagecoach," Slocum answered and saw the flash of anger on the lawman's face. "Where's your jurisdiction?"

"Most all the country above the White River to the Oglala grasslands. Now what's your name and what's your interest in this here supposedly missing stagecoach?"

"Name's Slocum, and I reckon my curiosity bump is bigger than yours if you're not looking for a stolen stage."

"Curiosity killed the cat, Slocum," the sheriff said. "Ain't no missing stagecoach."

"That answers my question," Slocum said. "Much obliged." He left quickly before the sheriff could ask more about him and his background. The question had turned the lawman prickly, just as his questions about the missing brewer had riled the bartender. The story looked to be the same wherever he went in northwestern Nebraska. Men—and stages—vanished and nobody talked about it.

Slocum mounted his Indian pony and tugged on the reins of his roan. The horse whinnied balefully but began clopping along, only to balk a ways outside of town. Turning to get a better grip on the bridle to pull the horse along, Slocum saw a settling dust cloud behind him. He had ridden so slowly neither of his horses had kicked up much fuss. Someone following him at a faster clip provoked the dust cloud.

Slocum whacked the roan's rump and got it moving along the road slowly, then trotted to a stand of lodgepole pines to see who was riding so fast behind him.

The man galloped past, only to jerk back hard on the reins, causing his horse to dig in its hooves. A newer, bigger cloud rose, momentarily obscuring the rider. When the brown curtain settled, Slocum got a better look at the man trailing him. The man stared at the solitary roan, not even carrying a pack or saddle, then went for his six-shooter. He swiveled around, hunting for Slocum. The pony Slocum rode let out a neigh at exactly the wrong time. The man spotted Slocum in the stand of trees, lifted his six-gun and fired.

The slug went high and blew splinters from the trunk of a pine tree. Slocum fought to keep the pony from bolting. This might be the reason Dark Cloud was so happy to give it away. A Blackfoot, even one in times of peace, could not afford a horse that shied around gunfire.

A second bullet whined closer to Slocum. He lowered his head, put his heels to the pony's flanks and rocketed forward. Controlling the horse was out of the question now, but Slocum's attack took the gunman by surprise. He raced forward, the man's horse now rearing to ruin his aim. As they passed, Slocum kicked free and crashed hard into the other rider. They fell heavily to the ground, but Slocum had a split second to anticipate the impact. He came to his feet, went into a crouch as his hand flashed for his six-shooter. Slocum never hesitated when it was obvious the downed gunman wasn't going to surrender.

Slocum cleared leather and fired, then fanned off three more quick rounds. The man on the ground thrashed about as if he had St. Vitus's dance, then he shuddered and dropped flat on his back. Slocum walked over, kicked the man's six-gun away and dropped to one knee to check his aim. Which of his bullets had taken the man's life was impossible to tell, but two were close enough to the heart to have done the deed.

Fishing through the man's pockets turned up a few greenbacks and a couple silver cartwheels, but nothing more. Slocum tucked those into his own shirt pocket, then grabbed the man's gun belt and heaved him up, caught him over his shoulders and staggered a few steps until he could drape the body across the man's saddle. His horse tried to rear, but Slocum held it down.

Climbing back into his own saddle, Slocum turned and headed back to town and the sheriff's office. He didn't even have to dismount. The burly sheriff lumbered out and stared at Slocum.

"What you been up to, Slocum? You didn't leave more 'n ten minutes ago and now you're back."

"He tried to kill me. Took two shots at me before I knocked him off his horse. He kept trying to kill me, so I did the honors."

"Jesus," the sheriff said barely loud enough for Slocum to hear. He had lifted the man's head enough to get a good look at his face.

"Who is it?"

"Jersey George McCoy."

"I've heard of him. He's wanted over in Omaha for bank robbery."

"Damned near every other town in Nebraska is lookin' for him, too," said the sheriff.

"What kind of reward is there for him?" Slocum asked. The paltry few dollars he had taken from the outlaw was hardly enough to reimburse him for the cost of the ammo used to end McCoy's vile life.

"Hunnerd dollars, probably," the sheriff said.

"What's your cut?" Slocum asked. It wasn't unknown for a lawman to take part of the reward for his own. They called their cut various things: handling fee; service charge; transaction expense. It all came down to the same thing. They wanted to be bribed not to pursue the details of the shooting too closely.

Giving the sheriff some of the money suited Slocum. The last thing he wanted was for the lawman to go pawing through a stack of wanted posters and find his face on it. After the war Slocum had returned to the family farm in Calhoun, Georgia, and had killed a carpetbagger judge trying to steal the land, citing "nonpayment of taxes." Ever since, Slocum had been dogged with the charge of murdering a federal judge. Moreover, Slocum had been less than lily-white in his dealings, sometimes crossing the line between the law and robbery.

But this time it had been a fair fight, and he had even given Jersey George McCoy a chance to surrender. For whatever reason, the outlaw had wanted nothing of it and had died for his mistake.

"No, sir, you ain't getting ole Jason Quince involved in this. I don't want any part of this. I never saw this varmint. You take him right out of town and you see him buried. The undertaker's long gone, but you can find a shovel out at the cemetery. You bury him."

"You aren't taking any of the reward?" Slocum repeated.

"I'll fetch you your blood money. I got discretionary

funds," Sheriff Quince said, spitting the words out syllable by syllable. "You bury McCoy and then you get the hell out of Nebraska."

The sheriff ducked back into the jailhouse and reappeared a few seconds later clutching a sheaf of greenbacks. Quince thrust it toward Slocum and said, "Here, take it. Take it and be damned. Now get on your horse and get the hell outta town!"

Slocum stuffed the money into his shirt pocket, mounted and led the horse with the outlaw's body in the direction the sheriff had pointed. He saw a small trail leading uphill and into a small meadow where tombstones and wooden crosses were spread haphazardly. Sure as rain, Quince had been right about a shovel leaning against a rock cairn by the entrance. Slocum had no desire to spend the time burying McCoy, but he considered the pay for it to be in his pocket. As he dug, he considered how peculiarly the sheriff had acted.

None of it made any sense. Slocum finally rolled the outlaw's body into the grave, refilled the hole and finally dusted off his hands. The sun was setting. Slocum knew he ought to hunt for the roan since it couldn't have wandered too far in its condition, but perhaps the horse was better off running free. The bridle might give it a bit of trouble but Slocum doubted it. He could look for the horse on his way back to Parson's Grove. In the morning.

He found himself a quiet spot near a small stream to bed down for the night and was on the trail at first light. He reached Parson's Grove sometime after noon and felt as if he had moved into a different world. The lethargy that had seized the town before now seemed like a frenzy. The main street was deserted, and he couldn't even see any horses tethered down side streets. He hadn't counted before, but he thought more stores were empty, just as in the town he had left the day before.

He kept a sharp lookout for Antoinette, but she spotted him first.

"John! Hello, over here!"

Slocum turned the pony's face and went to a small building set apart from the rest. He saw the sign and nodded. It was as he had expected.

"You're the new town doctor, aren't you?"

"I am, sir," Antoinette said proudly. "The former occupant of this surgery turned it over to me on his way back to Boston. He was in quite a hurry and left all his equipment." Antoinette sobered a little from her buoyant good humor and said, "I can use most of the equipment. I just hope there is no call to."

Slocum dismounted and went into the small office with the dark-haired woman. He looked around and saw she had put her mark on the office right away. He doubted the previous doctor had a vase filled with pale windflowers on the desk. Other small womanly touches removed the stark look usually found in such offices.

"Any customers yet?"

"Patients, John, patients."

"I try to be as patient as I can," he said. He had to laugh at her perplexed expression. "You notice anything happening around town I should know about?"

"Only that you didn't ride back with the same horse you rode out on."

Nothing got past Antoinette, but this wasn't the kind of information he needed.

"More people have left. Any gossip why?"

"I can't even find out what the baker's name was. They clam up when anything like that is mentioned. I think more of the people are packing up, ready to leave."

Slocum told her about the small town he had passed through and how it had been turned almost into a ghost town. He neglected to tell her of the strange ambush and shoot-out with McCoy because he knew that would only worry her needlessly.

"The entire region is frightened to death about something. Masked men in the middle of the night spiriting them away is one thing, but this goes deeper. Even the marshal lit out."

"I had a run-in with the sheriff back in that town, but he was hardly what I'd call a dedicated lawman."

"What are we going to do, John? The townspeople aren't beating their way to my door."

"Not yet. Wait a spell," Slocum said. "I'll do some more poking around. I have an idea how to find out the truth, but it might be a tad risky."

"Oh, and being a baker or livery owner isn't? In Parson's Grove, those are dangerous professions," Antoinette said, anger mounting. "I want you to do something. You know about all this. I want my Bible back. I want answers, John, I want it all."

Slocum realized the strain the woman had been under as she threw herself into his arms and hugged him close. He felt the hot, salty tears on his dusty shirt and let her paroxysms of frustration die down, then he lifted her chin with a forefinger, stared into her tear-filled blue eyes an instant and finally kissed her lightly.

"We'll work it out," Slocum said. "I promise."

"Why do I believe you?"

"Because you're a fool who ought to go back to Agate— or Fort Robinson—and wait for me."

"Oh, you," Antoinette said, pushing away from him. "Go do whatever you're going to do. I have to clean some of these surgical instruments. I declare, the doctor never saw a bit of rust he didn't want to keep for himself."

Slocum led his pony to the stables and put it in a stall. The young man running the livery was nowhere to be seen but the stalls had been mucked. Slocum tended the horse himself, made sure it had water and feed, then headed for the saloon. It hadn't been crowded before when he had been in Parson's Grove, but it was the only place where men's tongues loosened enough to say what was on their minds.

Slocum walked over to the front door of the saloon and looked in. He saw the barkeep talking with two men at the end of the bar. From the way they wore their six-shooters Slocum pegged them as gunslicks. The bartender was plenty scared of them but didn't flinch when first one, then the other asked him questions in a voice too low for Slocum to overhear. He pushed on through the doors and went to a spot halfway down the bar, head averted from the men.

"Beer," he ordered. The barkeep hardly looked at him as he drew the beer, dropped it in front of him and then returned to the end of the bar.

Slocum sipped the beer and turned so he could hear more without appearing to be eavesdropping.

"What about her? How long's she been in town?" demanded the first gunman, the one with a long pink scar across his cheek. The scar partially closed his left eye, giving him a squinty look.

"She just blew in the other day. Think she said she was from south. Down Agate way, she said."

"Why'd she come to Parson's Grove?" asked the second, a young buck with an arrogant look to him. Slocum had seen his kind before. Nobody told him anything, and the gunman usually had a hair trigger temper. This was the kind more likely to shoot his opponents in the back than face them.

"Maybe she heard there was a doctoring job here," the barkeep said.

The younger gunfighter moved with the speed of a striking rattler. He reached out and grabbed the barkeep by the throat and squeezed.

"The doc didn't leave town till she got here. You sayin' he wrote her to take his place?"

The bartender gurgled a little before the gunman released him.

"I don't know nuthin' 'bout her," the barkeep said, rubbing his throat. "Go ask her, if you gotta know all this stuff."

"She any good?" asked the scarred gunman in a pleasant, calm voice.

"Can't say. Nobody's needed to be patched up since she hung out her shingle. Antoinette Thibadeaux's her name. I remember her sayin' that. Reminded me of a whore from New Orleans I heard 'bout once."

"A New Orleans whore," mused the scarred gunfighter. "Now that's something we could use more 'n another doctor."

"Me first, Big Ed," the younger gunman said, laughing. "You can have her after I'm done with her."

"That'd be what, ten seconds?" The scarred gunman laughed, but Slocum knew this wasn't the sort of thing to say to the other man without angering him.

The younger gunman was quick, but Slocum was surprised at the scarred gunfighter's speed. He had his gun swinging before the young buck had his six-shooter half out of the holster. The barrel crashed into the young man's head and knocked him back. His knees buckled, but he never quite conked out.

"Get to your feet. We gotta do some travellin'," the older man said, holding his gun indolently, as if not sure why he had it in his hand. But from the way the muzzle never strayed much from the younger gunman's heart, a single quick tug on the trigger would end the discussion then and there.

"You hit me," moaned the young man.

"You damn well deserved it. Now get off your ass and come along." The scarred gunfighter shoved his six-shooter back into his holster, turned and walked from the saloon.

Slocum held his breath. If he had the younger man figured right, a bullet would blast apart the scarred man's spine. From where he stood at the bar Slocum couldn't get a good view of the injured gunman, but there was a long pause, then the man heaved himself to his feet. His six-shooter was still holstered, but Slocum had the feeling there had almost been a murder in the saloon.

Why the young man hadn't cut down his partner was yet another question without an answer. Slocum watched him stagger after his partner, then round the corner of the building and disappear from sight. Slocum downed his beer and hurried outside. From the way the two men were interrogating the barkeep, their only interest was Antoinette. Slocum wanted to know where they went—and if it was to Antoinette's, there'd be gunplay for certain.

Slocum chanced a quick glance around the corner of the building down the alley and saw the pair round the corner of the store next door. He hitched up his gun and headed after them, but Slocum only got to the back of the saloon when he heard a six-gun hammer coming back with a metallic click.

"Move a muscle and you're a dead man, Slocum."

Slocum came face-to-face with the sheriff he had left behind in the other town. The sheriff had his iron out and pointed straight at Slocum's face.

"You're under arrest for drunk and disorderly."

"I'm not drunk," Slocum said an instant before the sheriff hit him on the side of the head, causing him to stagger.

"You look mighty soused to me. Drunk and disorderly. Don't make me shoot you in the leg."

Dazed, Slocum couldn't prevent the lawman from plucking his Colt Navy from its holster and shoving him in the direction of the Parson's Grove jail.

8

Slocum lounged back against the brick wall, staring through the steel bars at Sheriff Quince. He had a crashing headache from where the lawman had buffaloed him, but the smoldering anger Slocum felt was what consumed him most.

"How long are you going to keep me locked up on those bogus charges?"

"Bogus? I saw you staggering around after coming out of a saloon, Slocum. That means you were drunk. Drunk and disorderly since you mouthed off to me when I said you were under arrest."

"Those are trumped up charges and you know it."

The sheriff came over and tugged at his bushy beard, nodding slowly.

"Yep, trumped up charges."

This took Slocum by surprise. He hadn't expected the man to admit it so readily.

"I did it for your own good. You're pokin' 'round where you shouldn't."

"How did you happen to be in Parson's Grove?" Slocum asked. "I thought you were holed up back in the town with no name."

"I asked around when you took McCoy to the boneyard

to get rid of his worthless carcass and found you was headin' here. Since this is part of my territory and I hadn't paid a visit to Parson's Grove in a month or so, I rode straight here."

"You knew the marshal had hightailed it?"

"Nope, but it don't surprise me much. Nielsen was a snake in the grass and spent more time arrestin' folks for stupid crimes so he could collect the fines. Hell and damnation, he was so dumb he taxed the whores out of business. They all left Parson's Grove months back."

"Some might think that was a good idea," Slocum said.

"Good? You ever seen a horny cowboy who's been on the range for a month or two, nothing but them cows and a peg boy or two, come to town lookin' to get laid and the whores are all gone? That's trouble. Big trouble."

"Parson's Grove looks peaceful enough." Slocum saw a cloud pass over the sheriff's face.

"There're other reasons nobody'll come here."

"Who am I supposed to pay my fine to?"

The sheriff laughed but there was scant humor in it.

"Keep your money." Sheriff Quince looked down and saw how Slocum tensed a little. "And I know you got that pig sticker in your boot. I wasn't lockin' you up to keep you for a long time or fine you. I did it to save your worthless life."

"Why?"

"Danged if I know. Might be I took a shine to you. More likely, I got tired of plantin' men like you out in the boneyard."

"That's why Parson's Grove and the other towns are disappearing? Anybody with a spine who stood up to them got gunned down?"

"That's about it," Quince said.

"Who're the ones doing all the killing?" Slocum asked.

"You killed McCoy. Those two I saved you from were Big Ed Lawrence and the Dakota Kid. Don't know any more of his name and don't want to. He's a real killer."

"The one with the scar?"

"That's Lawrence."

"The other one—the Dakota Kid—is the one to keep away from your back," Slocum said.

"Steer clear of them both. And they're not even the worst of that bunch."

Slocum saw he wasn't going to get any more information from the sheriff than he already had.

"When are you going to spring me?"

"Looks like it's 'bout time for dinner. Rather than feed you, since the cost'd come out of my pocket, I reckon you served your time and paid your debt to society." Sheriff Quince grabbed a ring of keys and turned one in the lock. It grated open with a rusty, grinding sound. The sheriff stepped back, drew Slocum's Colt from his belt and tossed it to him.

"That's a well-used gun. Take some advice. Don't use it 'round Parson's Grove. Don't even think of using it at all. Get on that pony of yours and clear out."

"You just might be giving me some good advice," Slocum said. The time he had spent in the cell cooling his heels had given him time to think about what he was doing. It rankled, but Slocum had come to the conclusion that finding Antoinette's Bible wasn't possible with most of northwestern Nebraska under the thumb of a gang of outlaws so dangerous they killed entire towns. The only answer he could come up with why men vanished in the night, as the baker had, was that they had somehow crossed the gang and were killed. Worse, the outlaws removed all trace of their families, too.

Slocum had been negligent getting the Thibadeaux Bible to Antoinette, but there were limits to what he could do. He had reached them.

"I'll be leaving town. Heading west."

"Nice Indian pony you got. When you find a town with a farrier, you might get it shod."

Slocum had not realized the sheriff was so observant.

He shouldn't have misjudged the lawman and yet he had. It was definitely time for him to move on.

Slocum settled his hat and stepped into the humid Nebraska night. His belly growled from lack of food, so Slocum decided to kill two birds with one stone. He'd take Antoinette to dinner and explain to her how he was giving up on the search for her family Bible. Then he would bid her good-bye. He hoped it would be amicable but if it wasn't, Slocum couldn't complain. They'd had some interesting days—and nights—together.

He walked past the restaurant and saw the waiter looking out a partly opened door, fearful as always. His stride lengthened as he made his way toward Antoinette's office, but it quickly turned into a run when he saw horses tethered to the side of the office.

Slocum whipped out his six-shooter as he ran, skidded to a halt in front of the doctor's office and peered through the window. The coal oil lamp inside had been turned down, but he made out a shadowy shape rummaging through the surgical equipment and tossing it helter-skelter into a sack. A quick glance around failed to show Slocum where Antoinette might be.

He kicked in the door. It slammed open on its hinges, then rebounded, coming back to block his shot at the masked man in the office.

"Drop it!" Slocum shouted, hoping to freeze the man for an instant. It didn't happen. The masked man went for a gun and opened fire. The foot-long orange tongues of flame blasting from the muzzle dazzled Slocum. It also gave him a target. He aimed just above the flame, figuring this was the biggest target he could hit in the darkness.

He was rewarded with a gasp, followed by a loud thud as the outlaw dropped his six-gun. Slocum kept firing and the man doubled over, then hobbled from the room. By the time Slocum's Colt came up empty he was fully in the office. He knelt, picked up the six-shooter dropped by the outlaw and followed into the examining room.

Slocum almost died when he was caught in a cross fire. Two other masked men, one in each corner of the room, opened up on him. Slocum lurched and fell forward, hitting his shoulder and dropping the captured pistol.

"Kill 'im. The son of a bitch shot me. I got hurt real bad," moaned a voice straight ahead of Slocum. That had to be the man who had rifled through the surgical equipment.

Slocum drew his knife, kept low and moved as quietly as possible. When he saw a leg in front of him, he stabbed out and was rewarded with another shriek of pain.

"He knifed me. He stuck me with a knife!"

Slocum slashed and drew blood again, but from the feel of the knife cutting through fabric and flesh, he knew he had inflicted only a scratch. Then Slocum gave up trying to mete out any further damage to the thief. The other two walked toward him, firing as they came. Slocum rolled under the examining table and felt something hard under his back. Reaching around, his fingers closed on the fallen pistol.

He swung it around and fired wildly. Three quick shots at the advancing legs brought another shriek of pain. The fourth time the hammer fell on a spent chamber.

"Damnation, hc shot mc, too."

"Get out, get out of here!"

Slocum heard boots hammering against the wood floor and then a scuffle outside. He recognized the voice and, in spite of not having a loaded gun, rushed to the rear door.

"Antoinette!" he shouted. Slocum saw four riders galloping away, one smaller than the others. He fancied he saw her long dark hair pulling away from her face as she rode, but it might have been an illusion. Still, Slocum was positive the three had kidnapped Antoinette Thibadeaux.

He threw down the captured six-shooter and worked to reload his Colt as he walked to the livery stable. Not once along the way did he consider letting Sheriff Quince know what had happened. If the gunfire hadn't brought the lawman running, a story of kidnaping certainly wouldn't budge him from the otherwise abandoned marshal's office.

Slocum stormed into the stables, grabbed his saddle and dropped it on the pony. The horse protested the lack of rest but had heart and responded quickly to Slocum's urging to gallop after the kidnappers. His only hope was that Antoinette's struggles would slow them and give him a chance to overtake the trio of owlhoots.

After a few minutes of frantic galloping, Slocum slowed to a walk and then came to a dead halt. He let the horse rest as he turned this way and that, listening hard for sounds of the kidnappers. They made no sound but Antoinette succeeded in letting out a squeal that allowed Slocum to home in on them. He turned in that direction. In the darkness one way looked like another. Clouds had silently blotted out the stars, and there wasn't a moon worth mentioning. Slocum had to advance in inky darkness, but the pony's surefooted gait allowed him to prepare for the fight.

He double-checked his six-shooter and made sure all the chambers were loaded. Then he drew the Winchester from its scabbard and pressed in on the magazine cover to reveal the end of a cartridge. The magazine was crammed to capacity. Slocum was ready for a fight.

All he had to do was make certain Antoinette wasn't hurt during the shooting. He had shot and cut one outlaw and probably wounded another in the leg. That reduced the odds against him considerably. The first owlhoot wouldn't put up any kind of a fight, not with leg cuts and a couple rounds to his chest or belly. The second likely couldn't walk without a serious limp. Those two would remain on their horses to give them mobility. If they planned any kind of an ambush for him, the third man was the one who'd draw that card.

Slocum got his bearings again as Antoinette cried out, only to be muffled quickly. A muttered curse told Slocum she had bitten her captor. If only she could make a break, the kidnappers would be at his mercy. Slocum could shoot them without fear of hitting her. But from the sounds ahead, he guessed they had subdued her, probably gagging and hog-tying her.

They might not be smart enough to use her outcry as bait, but Slocum pretended they were and that the uninjured kidnapper was ready with a rifle to potshoot anyone coming up the trail. Slocum cut to the right and made a wide circle so he would approach from their flank. The going got rough mighty fast when he had to go up and down steep ravines, then exit into a grove of stunted oak trees. He saw that riding farther wouldn't get him anywhere without making a passel of noise.

Slocum slid to the ground, took his rifle and advanced slowly, estimating where the one uninjured outlaw would have set up his ambush. Slocum wanted to tackle the two injured men, the ones guarding Antoinette. He went into a crouch and duckwalked forward, avoiding the low bushes and thorny vegetation as he went. A patch of prickly pear cactus forced him to make a wider circle than anticipated, but he didn't want the spines getting into his hide and distracting him when the shooting started.

And it would. He would take the trio out and to hell with finding out what their plans for Antoinette were. Deep down he knew it was more than simple kidnaping and rape that was on the men's minds, but what else didn't matter now.

Between two tall, straight trees he saw them. One stood on either side of Antoinette, one holding her and the other braced against a rock, clutching his six-gun. Slocum drew a bead on one, then hesitated. Antoinette was struggling. He didn't want to hit her by accident.

Realizing he needed a different angle, Slocum backtracked and then found a spot where he could get clean shots at both men.

". . . get to the valley 'fore sundown tomorrow?" asked one.

"No way. We got to fight this spitfire all the way. I still think we should throw a lasso around her ankles and drag her a spell. That'd take some of the piss and vinegar out of her." The outlaw poked Antoinette with his six-shooter. She squealed and tried to lash out, but the outlaws had her too tightly bound and gagged. She fought for a few seconds, then subsided.

Slocum's finger drew back on the trigger, but he hesitated short of firing when the first man spoke.

"How much longer we gotta kidnap people? We got a whole damned town of 'em now."

"You know what the boss said. We got to keep our womenfolk happy. And this one can teach some of the kids, too. She was a schoolmarm down in Agate. Remember when we were there a couple weeks back?"

The question made sense to Slocum but the answer didn't. He shrugged it off. It was time to go to work. He settled the rifle against his shoulder, aimed and started to pull back on the trigger when he heard a twig snap behind him. Before he could either fire or roll over and defend himself, something hard and heavy smashed into the back of his head.

He half came to, his belly over a saddle as he jostled along. He tried to lift his head enough to see where he was, where they were going. He caught a hint of pink in the sky. Dawn. He had been unconscious for hours. Then he gave up the effort and sagged back, letting the horse bounce him around as blackness enveloped him again.

When he awoke the next time, his head felt like a rotted melon. He moaned softly and touched the back of his head. The fingers came away with a smear of new blood mixed with dry, crusty blood. He rolled over onto his side and stared. It took him a few seconds to realize he was inches away from a stone wall. Repositioning himself slowly, he rolled the other way and blinked hard to get his eyes clear and his senses responding.

He was back in the Parson's Grove jail, but the cell door hadn't been locked this time. Beyond the iron bars he saw Sheriff Quince gesturing and trying to make a point.

Slocum couldn't see who the lawman spoke to. Eventually the words drifted back to him.

"He's a meddler. Put him somewhere he can't bother us again."

The voice of the unseen man sounded, deeply resonant and almost familiar. Slocum rubbed the back of his head when new lightning blasts of pain shot through it.

"You messed everything up tonight. Where do we go from here?"

"You're asking me? This is your operation!" Quince cried. He waved his arms around in agitation. "There's nothin' goin' right 'round here, nothin'! And you're tellin' *me* to do something. This is your show. You're the one who insisted on that from the start!"

Slocum tried to hear the rest but his head began throbbing like a tooth with a raw nerve. His ears roared and he couldn't help himself when he let out a soft moan of pain. This brought Quince back to the cell.

"So you're comin' 'round, are you? Too bad."

The sheriff took two quick steps into the cell. Slocum never saw the pistol butt that crashed down onto his head. The world went away again.

9

Slocum sneezed. When he sneezed again so hard that it hurt, he struggled to see where he was. His head hurt like he had been on a three-day drunk but the dust caused him the most misery. Coughing, he sat up and brushed it off. He had been dumped into a grain bin in a stable. From the way the light sneaked through the walls, he wasn't in the livery in town. That had been well constructed in comparison to these flimsy walls. As if to verify his opinion, he reached out to support himself as he stood and the board in the wall came unnailed.

Woozy from being knocked out so many times, he staggered through the filthy stables and out into the bright Nebraska sun. The sky was clouding up, promising rain that had been denied for weeks, but the air still hung heavy and listless. After he plunged his head into a water barrel and shocked himself back to full awareness, he reached for his Colt Navy. To his surprise, it hung in his holster as if it had never been out. Going back into the stables, he hunted for his pony.

It wasn't there.

Slocum checked his shirt pocket to see if his money had been stolen, too, but the wad of greenbacks was as thick as it had ever been. Then Slocum counted through the bills and found it came up twelve dollars shy, but someone had put a stagecoach ticket in the pocket. A twelve-dollar ticket.

"Way station," Slocum said, his brain finally delivering answers to the pieces of the world around him. He had awakened in the barn of a way station.

Going back outside he circled the barn and saw the way station twenty yards off. He walked to it on increasingly steady legs. Sitting in the shade on the front porch was an old man who spat toward a cuspidor at the end of the porch, occasionally scoring a bull's-eye but more often missing from the brown stains on the wood around the brass pot.

"Howdy, mister," he greeted. "Wondered when you'd be around to claim your ride."

"My ride?"

"You got a ticket, you get to ride on the Butterfield Stagecoach Linc."

Slocum took out the ticket and looked at it. The sweat-smudged destination read Omaha. He didn't want to go to Omaha. He had to rescue Antoinette Thibadeaux—and get back his horse. And extract a measure of justice for all that had been done to him. He didn't know who all might be responsible, but he knew where to start.

Sheriff Quince back in Parson's Grove had a powerful lot of explaining to do.

"Mind if I pull up a chair?" Slocum asked.

"Do what suits you. We got a spell to wait 'til the stage comes through."

"How long?"

"For Omaha, it won't be 'til tomorrow noon. Maybe later, depending on how good the horses are feelin'."

"Any heading toward Parson's Grove?" Slocum didn't have a good idea where he was, but he hadn't been unconscious long enough to be too far from town.

"I ain't supposed to let you go back that way. Got orders."

"From Sheriff Quince?"

"Now, boy, I got to keep my secrets. Ain't got nothin' else out here but secrets to keep. Ever since the missus died, been lonely but at least I don't have to worry about sayin' what I shouldn't. She had a way of gettin' everything out of me, she did. Yes, sir, I do miss her. Gone a year next month. Or will it be two years?"

Slocum considered making the old man tell him who had dumped him out here, but decided it wasn't worth the effort. The station master might name men Slocum had no knowledge of. Whatever had gone on, he had to start with Sheriff Quince and go from there.

"Must get lonely out here," Slocum said. "That's good. Gives a man time to think."

"Most of the time, it's the medicine the doctor ordered. Get to say howdy to the passengers and drivers, sell them some food for their trip, then come on back here and watch the clouds go by. I like watching the clouds most of all."

"You worry much about the road agents working the line?" Slocum asked.

"Do I look like a damn fool? 'Course I worry about them. They hold up three or four stages a month. The home office cain't abide by such losses, but there's nothin' they kin do. Put more guards on the stage and they don't get held up."

"So they know which stagecoaches to rob?"

"Hell, boy, sometimes they do more 'n steal the mail and whatever's in the strongbox. Sometimes they steal the whole damn coach. Done that a half dozen times in the past year."

"That long? They've been robbing the Butterfield Line that long?"

"Longer, but it's only got worse. The law's good for nothin'. Most of the town marshals are history, the spineless yellow-bellies. There's a deputy federal marshal somewhere in the area, but I don't know where."

"What about Sheriff Quince?"

"He's a good man," the station master said carefully. He

spat and missed. Slocum took this to mean he was a bit disconcerted at the mention of the name of the lawman who had left an unwanted visitor in his barn.

"Can't the cavalry do anything about the robberies? I was at Fort Robinson a while back, and they have a full regiment there."

"Yankees, the lot of 'em," grumbled the station master. This time when he spat, his aim was dead center of the spittoon.

"They have their hands full with the Sioux. Might be another uprising in the cards," said Slocum.

"Always is. They have to keep them redskins in their place, but more 'n that, they oughta stop them road agents from shootin' up my stagecoaches."

In the distance Slocum saw a cloud of dust rising and pointed.

"That's the stage a 'comin' now," the old geezer said squinting against the bright sunlight. "Ain't for you, though."

"I wasn't supposed to wake up until this stage had gone, was I?"

"That was what I was told."

"There'd be a difference in cost for a ticket to Omaha rather than to Parson's Grove, wouldn't there?"

"Don't expect me to refund the difference. Don't keep company money out here. I'd be a sittin' duck for them robbers. Besides, the home office don't trust me with money, not with folks pulling up stakes and movin' on so fast in these parts. Don't know there'd be anywhere I'd go that was better 'n here, though."

Slocum started to feel good about the arrangement when the station master spat again, and said "'Course, you gettin' on *that* stage ain't gonna get you to Parson's Grove."

"Why not? You can't stop me."

"Don't figure on it. My achin' joints notwithstandin', on my best day when I was a stripling I couldna gone against you. Well, maybe a round or two." The station master spit, hitting dead center and causing a ringing that could be heard a mile off. He wiped his lips and went on. "Fact is, that stage don't ever go to Parson's Grove, not from here. That's the stage for Scott's Bluff."

"Then I'll head for Scott's Bluff," Slocum said.

"Be my guest. Don't get no refund on your ticket."

"That's all right," Slocum said, wishing he had a bottle of whiskey about now. His head ached something fierce and the ride into Scott's Bluff wasn't going to do him any good. He stood and waited for the stage to pull up. The driver and shotgun messenger jumped down and made short work of swapping the team with one the station master had waiting in a small corral nearby.

"You goin' on into Scott's Bluff?" asked the driver. Slocum silently handed him the ticket. The driver frowned, started to say something but looked at the station master. Slocum wasn't sure what silent communication flowed between them but the driver growled, "Go on, git in. We're tryin' to make up danged near an hour's time lost back at a ravine."

"What happened?" Slocum asked as he stepped up to the coach.

"Road washed out. Imagine that. Clear sky and the ravine was runnin' full. Musta rained cats and dogs up in the hills for so much runoff to wipe out part of the road. Hang on, mister, we're gonna fly!"

Slocum kept from screaming as the coach swayed from side to side and endeavored to hit every pothole and rock in the road, but by the time they reached Scott's Bluff, the pain in his head had died down to a dull ache. Nothing a few shots of whiskey wouldn't cure. Walking carefully to keep from jolting his head too much, Slocum went into the first saloon he saw.

A bored woman in a skimpy dress tried to interest him in a game of faro, but Slocum wanted nothing more than to make the pain go away. He owed Sheriff Quince for at least one of those blows on the head and as he had ridden into Scott's Bluff, decided he might have all of them to lay at the lawman's door.

"What can I do for you?" asked another pretty waiter girl. Slocum hardly looked at her as he ordered. "You want some company with that?"

"I want a glass with that," he said more sharply than necessary.

"Grouch," she said, sashaying away, making sure he got a good look at the hitch in her get-along to let him know what he was passing up. As far as Slocum was concerned he wanted no part of the gambling or the women.

The first shot of whiskey almost convinced him he didn't want any liquor, either. But the second shot went down a little easier, and by the time he had polished off a half bottle he was feeling almost human again. The dull throb in his head had vanished, and the aches and pains in his body were well hidden behind an alcoholic haze.

He looked around the saloon and saw that they had a decent enough sized crowd for early in the evening. He wondered if any of the gang making their hideout up in the Black Hills ever came into Scott's Bluff to carouse. Somehow he doubted it. They preyed on smaller towns, with only one lawman and citizens too scared to defend themselves. A town the size of Scott's Bluff would have half a dozen deputies and enough businessmen with much to lose that they could form a posse and go after the kidnappers.

Slocum nursed the rest of his liquor, thinking on what he had overheard. Antoinette's captors had hinted that there was an entire town somewhere up in the hills. Other than being a beautiful woman, Antoinette also had skills that would be mighty useful. She could doctor and she could teach.

He jerked around when a commotion started at the far end of the bar. For a split second Slocum thought he saw the Dakota Kid, but it proved to be a drunken cowboy come to town to blow off a little steam. The youngster wasn't even wearing a six-gun. Slocum doubted the Dakota Kid ever took his off, even to bathe, if he bothered. When he was finally planted in the ground he would still have his six-shooter strapped around his waist.

Slocum heaved to his feet, got his balance, then walked from the saloon and looked up and down the street. He got his bearings and headed for the marshal's office. The marshal was out making the rounds but had left a deputy in charge. The lawman glanced up from the newspaper he had spread in front of him on the desk.

"What kin I do fer ya?"

"Mind if I paw through your wanted posters?"

"You a bounty hunter?"

"Nope," Slocum said. "I'm looking for someone in particular, and he's likely to have his face on one of your posters."

"Hep yersef," the deputy said, jerking his thumb over his shoulder in the direction of a cabinet where a foot-high stack of posters rested. Slocum heaved a deep breath, took the posters and began leafing through them.

When he came to Jersey George McCoy he stopped and read the details. Quince had played fair. The reward for McCoy, dead or alive, was one hundred dollars. Slocum put that poster aside and began looking for others that mentioned McCoy as an accomplice or outright partner. He wasn't too surprised to find both the Dakota Kid and Ed Lawrence peering up at him, their ugly faces even more menacing in the pictures. Putting those aside, he built a small pile of a half dozen others, all with interlocking arrests with those men. The best he could tell, someone named Will Arno was their leader, but there wasn't a poster with a likeness of him on it, either photographed or sketched by an artist. That probably meant Arno was a long sight smarter than the others and had never been caught. Yet.

"You findin' what yer lookin' fer?" asked the deputy, finally finished with his newspaper. He folded it meticulously and placed it to one side of the desk. Slocum wondered if the deputy had read the marshal's paper and didn't want his boss knowing about it.

"Got a few I'm interested in."

The deputy half rose from the chair and peered down at the wanted posters. He let out a snort.

"Quite a rogue's gallery ya got there. Don't go crossin' none of them backshooters, not unless you got a company of cavalry soldiers with you. Even then, it might be downright dangerous."

"You know if any of them are in the area?"

The deputy shook his head.

"Hope to God none of 'em are. Takin' care of drunks is more 'n enough work fer me."

He sat back down and stared at Slocum, as if memorizing every line in his face, every gesture, every thought that might ooze from his cracked skull.

"Much obliged," Slocum said. He had a half dozen other faces to go along with Lawrence and the Dakota Kid. Whether he ran into any of them hardly mattered, but he suspected he would when he tracked them down and rescued Antoinette Thibadeaux.

It was always good to know who he was shooting.

10

Slocum waited impatiently for the stage bound for Parson's Grove to arrive. He had exhausted the sources of information in Scott's Bluff and was anxious to get his pony back and head out hunting the outlaw gang that had kidnapped Antoinette. As he paced back and forth, his mind raced on the possibilities. He had enough money to outfit himself for a considerable hunt in the Black Hills. With so many outlaws apparently availing themselves of its protection, the hideout could not be hard to find. Slocum had seen similar places where outlaws roosted.

They might not be hard to find but they could be hard to rout out. With so many in the gang—or taking advantage of the sanctuary Will Arno provided—he would be facing dozens of gunmen.

"Can't go at them head-on," he decided. Better to sneak in, free Antoinette and then get the hell out. Let the law go after Arno and his cronies. As that thought crossed his mind, he snorted in contempt. The town marshals were beyond their jurisdiction, as well as their ability to enforce the laws. Arno and his gang might be on Sheriff Quince's platter, but Slocum wasn't sure that the sheriff wasn't securely in Arno's hip pocket. The times the lawman had bashed Slocum on the head were becoming legion and the snippets Slocum remembered all pointed to Quince not wanting to do much to bring the outlaws to justice. He had been arguing with someone about Slocum poking his nose into the outlaws' business. Slocum fought to remember the sound of that voice chewing out Quince but couldn't. He had heard it before, somewhere, some time, before he had his head bashed in too many times.

In a way, Slocum didn't fault Quince for that. Arno had assembled a mighty big band of road agents if he preyed on entire towns and stole stagecoaches for his own amusement. Still, it was Quince's duty to keep the peace, and he was falling down on the job. Slocum figured he might be collecting a sizable bribe every now and then from the outlaw boss to look the other way. That was why Quince hadn't wanted any part of the reward when Slocum had cut down Jersey George McCoy. To have taken any part of it would have marked him as openly opposing the outlaws and put him in jeopardy.

Slocum considered alerting the commander at Fort Robinson about his little excursion into the hills to rescue Antoinette but decided against it. While the Army had the manpower to fight the outlaws, he suspected their orders dealt more with the Sioux uprising than a few robbed stagecoaches or citizens missing from their jobs in hole-in-the-wall towns.

"Here she comes!" cried the ticket agent, coming onto the boardwalk. "Y'all got yer tickets?"

Slocum had not noticed the other passenger, a tall, gaunt man wearing a tall Lincolnesque silk hat and long black broadcloth coat. The man tucked a Bible under his arm and passed over a ticket. Slocum pulled the one he had purchased earlier and gave it to the agent.

"He the only other passenger?" Slocum asked.

"Goin' to Parson's Grove? He surely is. Reckon he liked the name."

"How's that?" Slocum asked. Then he got the joke. The man was probably a parson on his way to Parson's Grove.

"Going my way, brother?" asked the parson.

"Seems we have a common destination," Slocum said. The man of the cloth looked Slocum over, from head to toe and shook his head sadly.

"I doubt that is so, but it can be if you change your ways." He held the Bible in front of him as if it were a shield against Slocum's worldliness. For him it might be enough to defend against the evils of the world, but Slocum preferred his trusty six-shooter.

"Climb on in. They done got a fresh team just outside o' town," the ticket agent said.

From the driver's box, the shotgun guard called down, "Don't go makin' promises you can't keep, Jess. We got one horse that's pullin' up lame. It'll be a couple minutes while we check."

The driver lashed the reins around the hand brake and jumped down. The guard made his way to the top of the stage and looked around town, hunting for any sign of trouble.

"Should we wait in the coach?" asked the parson.

"Suit yerse'f," the ticket agent said. "They'll let you know when they's 'bout ready to pull out."

"After you, sir," the parson said, indicating that Slocum should precede him, but Slocum had taken the shotgun guard's diligence to heart and took a gander at the people nearby. His heart skipped a beat when he spotted the Dakota Kid lounging indolently across the street, picking his teeth with the tip of a large-bladed knife.

Slocum stepped to one side and put a post between him and the Kid so he could search for others. Not ten yards away, also on the far side of the street, Big Ed Lawrence sat in a chair by a pickle barrel, looking as if he didn't have a care in the world. But now and then his eyes darted in the direction of the stagecoach, and Slocum knew the pair was waiting to give the signal that the coach was leaving town.

He considered calling to the guard atop the stagecoach to warn him. But he had other fish to fry. Slocum didn't care as much about the stage being robbed as he did about finding Antoinette. And either of the outlaws across the street could tell him where she had been taken and possibly get him into Will Arno's hideout—with a six-gun at their heads, if necessary.

Slocum ducked back of the stage depot and ran to the far side of a building on the other side. He wanted to come up on Lawrence from his blind side, preferring to let the Dakota Kid continue watching the stage. As he hurried along Slocum wondered what was on the stage that drew the two outlaws' attention. It had to be something already loaded aboard, probably a strongbox filled with money for the Parson's Grove bank or something in the mailbag.

He dashed across the street, caught sight of Lawrence still sitting and eating his pickle, then went to the rear of the general store and made his way through the crowded interior to come out beside the gunman.

Slocum slipped his six-shooter from its holster and popped through the front door, the muzzle pointing at the chair . . . where Lawrence had been sitting. In the time it had taken Slocum to go through the store from the rear, the outlaw had disappeared. Slocum swung around, pistol levelled and ready to fire but he couldn't find a decent target. The Dakota Kid had also ducked from sight.

Considering where they must have gone, Slocum crossed the street and kept going until he came out behind the stage depot again. Both men had their heads together, whispering furiously. It looked to be another of their interminable arguments. Slocum wasn't keen on taking them both on at the same time but had no choice. The Kid had already spotted him and was going for his smoke wagon.

Slocum knew the Dakota Kid wasn't too bright from the instant he had first laid eyes on him. Trying to throw down on a man when his six-gun was already pointed at your heart was a big mistake. Slocum fired before the Kid could get his six-shooter clear of his holster. The shot only winged the gunman, spinning him around to smash into the rear wall of the stage depot, but it put him out of action.

"Don't try it, Lawrence," Slocum called. "I'll cut you down where you stand."

The scar-faced outlaw lifted his hands and turned slowly to get a better look at his captor. The puckered scar gave him an evil aspect, but Slocum was in no mood to be intimidated by the glare he got.

"Thought we'd killed you," Lawrence said.

"You were wrong. I want—" That was as far as Slocum got in making his demand for information about Antoinette Thibadeaux. The Dakota Kid had slipped down to his knees, his face and hands hidden until he suddenly spun and fired a derringer in Slocum's direction. The heavy slug ripped a hole in Slocum's hat and sent it flying. Involuntarily flinching at the closeness of the bullet, Slocum made the mistake of letting his muzzle drift from dead center of Lawrence's chest rather than killing the man outright.

This was all the opening the road agent needed to draw and fire. Slocum had to admit that the scar-faced man was quick. But speed was less important than marksmanship. Lawrence fired and his slug went a foot or more to Slocum's right. The Kid had been more accurate with his hideout derringer than Lawrence was with his Colt.

Slocum fired but was off-balance and missed both of them. Then he had to take cover because both the Kid and Lawrence got their six-shooters blazing. Chunks of brick flew from the building behind him as their bullets smashed into the wall. Slocum flopped on his belly and wiggled forward, getting behind the dubious shelter offered by a crosspiece from a yoke left to rot.

Resting his Colt on the splintery wood crosspiece, Slocum fired twice more but he was shooting at empty air. Lawrence had slipped his arm around the Dakota Kid's shoulders and pulled him around the side of the depot, out of the line of fire.

Slocum scrambled to his knees, alert for a trap. When

he didn't see either man make the quick look around the edge of the depot to take a shot, he threw caution to the winds and ran straight ahead, his pistol pointed in the direction of the building's corner. He crashed into the back wall, took a deep breath and whirled around, ready to shoot both the Kid and Lawrence.

The two had hightailed it, not even slowing in their retreat to take a last shot at him. Slocum ran into the street and looked around. The driver and shotgun guard turned their attention toward him, but Slocum wasn't in any mood to explain.

"Where'd they go? Two men coming from beside the depot?"

"That way," the guard said, indicating farther down the street with the muzzle of his shotgun. "You shoot one of 'em?"

Slocum was already pounding down the dusty street, hunting for the two outlaws. They were his ticket into Arnot's hideout or at least they could give him what he needed to know about Antoinette's whereabouts.

Panting harshly, Slocum slowed his headlong rush and looked around, worrying that the two had staked out a spot to ambush him. In the middle of a town as bustling as Scott's Bluff, bystanders would get themselves shot up if that happened. But try as he might, Slocum couldn't spot either of the men. He looked at the street and tried to pick up any blood drops left by the Kid. The thirsty ground must have soaked it up completely. Or the Kid's wound wasn't as bad as Slocum hoped.

"Where's the livery stable?" Slocum asked of a man who had stopped to stare at him.

"D-down there. T-two blocks and then left."

Slocum realized he had his six-gun pointed at the man.

"Thanks," he said, running as fast he could now. If the outlaws had left their horses at the stable, they'd had plenty of time to get there. They hadn't shown any inclination to stand and fight, making him think they were more likely to be on their horses going out of town now than waiting for him.

"Stop!" Slocum shouted when he saw the two road agents leaving a barn. He took aim and fired. The hammer fell on a dud. He quickly cocked the Colt again and fired, but the distance was too great now. He missed both men as they galloped off.

Slocum slammed his iron back into the cross-draw holster and ran into the livery looking around for any horse he could take to give chase.

"What the hell's goin' on?" came the gruff question. Slocum jerked around and found himself staring into the twin barrels of a shotgun.

"I need a horse. Those two owlhoots who rode out are road agents."

"Don't know about that, but I do know they paid. You have the look of a man intendin' to steal a horse."

"I can pay. I need a horse and tack," Slocum said.

"You jist slow down, mister. There's no hurry."

Slocum wasn't so sure of that. He was continually astounded at how Lawrence and his partner turned to smoke and simply disappeared. The best chance he was likely to get to find Antoinette was going with them into oblivion.

"Don't!" the man with the double-barreled shotgun warned, poking it in Slocum's direction as he started for his six-gun.

"It's all right," Slocum said. "You have a horse and gear for sale?"

"Might, fer the right price." The shotgun muzzle never wavered as it followed Slocum through the stables.

"This one?"

"Fifty dollars," the man said. "I'll throw in a saddle and bridle for another fifty."

"Too much," Slocum said. He chafed at the delay, then realized any chance he had of catching the two outlaws had slipped through his fingers. His best bet was to get on the stagecoach and wait for them to hold it up. He could warn the driver and guard and lay a trap for Lawrence and the Kid.

"I'll get back to you on the horse and tack," Slocum said, hands up where the man could see them as he backed away. When he turned and left the barn the hair on the back of his neck prickled. He knew the livery owner still had that scattergun trained on him.

Slocum's luck continued to run bad. He returned to the depot only to find the stagecoach gone.

"Where is it?" he called to the ticket agent, now behind his window with his feet hiked up to the window ledge.

"The stage? It done left, that's where it is. You missed 'er. But another one'll be leavin' fer Parson's Grove in a couple days."

"It's going to be robbed," Slocum said. "Go fetch the marshal and tell him Big Ed Lawrence and the Dakota Kid are going to rob your stage."

"You ain't kiddin', are ya?" The agent's eyes went wide. "Them road agents are gonna be the death of me yet."

"They'll be the death of the driver, guard and all the passengers."

"Only that parson was ridin' inside," the agent said.

"You've got horses out back in the corral. Let me take one and go after the stage. I might reach them before the road agents so I can warn them. You tell the marshal and get as big a posse as you can on the trail."

"If you're wrong, I'm gonna look plenty foolish."

"If I'm right and you don't do anything, you'll have the blood of three men on your hands."

"Head office wouldn't like another robbery," the agent said, mulling over the matter. He looked back at Slocum. "You saw it was Big Ed Lawrence and who?"

"The Dakota Kid."

"Heard of 'em. All right, I'll tell the marshal. And you take the paint. It's the only one of them cayuses that's saddle-broke, too."

As the agent ambled off to tell the marshal, Slocum ran

around back. He took time to reload his six-shooter, then he cut the paint from the corral, got a saddle and cinched it down tight. The horse didn't cotton much to having the girth around its middle after pulling a stage but the agent was right. The horse didn't protest hardly at all when Slocum mounted.

"Run, damn you, run!" Slocum cried, putting his heels to the horse's flanks. The horse shot off like a rocket. Slocum hunched down and let the horse carry him along the road to Parson's Grove. He hadn't been entirely honest with the station agent in detailing who the road agents might be, but there hadn't been time to explain.

Slocum doubted either Lawrence or his partner would be capable of a holdup right now, not with the Kid carrying around a slug in him. But he was sure they had been scouts and nothing more. When they spotted what the gang wanted on the stagecoach, they relayed the information to others who would conduct the actual robbery. Slocum knew he might be up against a dozen or more of Arnot's gang, but he didn't care. He had to capture one of them to find where they had taken Antoinette. Barring that, he could follow the gang to their hideout and extricate Antoinette.

The stage couldn't be more than fifteen or twenty minutes ahead of him down the road. He doubted Arnot intended to rob the stage that close to Scott's Bluff, but the outlaw leader was getting cocky. The way he waltzed into smaller towns and boldly kidnapped his victims told that.

As Scott's Bluff vanished behind him on the road Slocum heard gunshots ahead. His paint was beginning to falter. He had forgotten that the horse had helped pull the stage into Scott's Bluff and was already tired. If he pushed it any harder, it might collapse under him. Cursing, Slocum slowed the pace until the horse was stumbling along at hardly a walk. Its flanks were lathered and it tossed its head, as if wanting to bolt. The gunfire from ahead refused to die down. Slocum took that as a good sign. The guard and the driver were putting up quite a fight.

But even as the thought crossed his mind, the last of the gunshots echoed away to nothing through the hilly country. Either the pair had surrendered or been killed.

Slocum saw how the road twisted and turned in an oxbow. To save time he cut across country, having to negotiate a sudden ravine and then the steeper slope on the far side. But when he came to more level ground he was again on the road and had the stagecoach in sight.

This time the outlaws hadn't bothered stealing it, too, but Slocum saw the door to the passenger compartment swinging open in the hot breeze blowing down from the Black Hills. He drew his Colt and rode forward, wary of a trap.

When he saw movement, he brought his pistol up and aimed, then lowered the hammer. The guard had flopped on his belly atop the stage and had risen up enough to see who approached.

"They got the preacher man. They took 'im!" the shotgun guard croaked out. "Why'd they want a preacher?"

"What happened to the driver?"

"Knocked out. Bullet caught him on the side of the head. I can hear him wheezin' so he's not dead. And he's still bleedin' like a stuck pig, but it's nothin' serious."

"What about you?" Slocum was torn between helping the men and getting on the trail. With any luck he might rescue the parson—or at least get a good idea where the gang was headed. They couldn't make as fast a getaway with their captive as they could without him.

"Winged. My arm's hurtin' somethin' fierce," the guard said, sitting with his legs dangling over the top of the stage and kicking slowly so his heels banged into the wooden side.

"If you're going to be all right, I'll go after them."

"You might want to take this. Ain't doin' me no good." The guard clumsily tossed Slocum his shotgun.

"Shells?"

"Dang, fergot 'bout them. Got a box somewhere." The guard flopped around like a fish out of water as he pushed things out of the way in the foot well of the driver's box.

"Never mind. I'll use my six-shooter."

"Who's that comin'? More of them varmints?" The guard poked his head up into the air like a prairie dog on sentry duty. "Must be eight or ten of 'em, all ridin' fast."

"Did they take the mailbag?"

"Hell and damnation, all they took was the preacher man. You reckon they's comin' back for the mail? Gimme back my scattergun!"

Slocum tossed it to him but knew any chance of pursuing the parson was gone now. He had to stay and make a stand against the rest of the road agents. Slocum wheeled his paint around and drew a bead on the spot in the road where the first rider would appear.

As the horseman came galloping up, Slocum lifted his six-gun and lowered the hammer. He caught the glint of sunlight off a badge. This was the posse from town he had told the station agent to send.

"Marshal, I'm surely glad to see yer ugly face," the guard said, standing up on the roof of the stage and wobbling a mite. "They done shot that fool driver of mine."

"What about this one?" The marshal pointed at Slocum.

"He come ridin' up a minute or two after the rest of them owlhoots lit out. He was tryin' to save the parson."

"You the one who told Jess to fetch me?" the marshal asked.

Slocum nodded.

"You knew there was gonna be a robbery? How?"

"I spotted the Dakota Kid and Ed Lawrence in town. I put a bullet into the Kid but they got away. The only reason they'd be hanging around the stage depot was if they were going to tell the rest of their gang to stick it up."

"Makes sense," the marshal said. "Let's git on back to town so we can talk on it a bit more."

"They're getting away," Slocum protested. "With the preacher. They kidnapped him!"

"More important right now to get the stage back where it belongs. The mailbag intact?"

"Surely is, Marshal," the guard said. "Some of you boys want to get him down into the passenger coach?" The guard pointed to the driver curled up in the box. "He's in no condition to drive. Neither am I." The guard used his left hand to raise his right arm. Blood dripped from it onto the roof of the stagecoach.

"Do as he says," the marshal ordered two of his deputies. He turned a gimlet stare on Slocum and asked, "You know to drive a rig like this?"

Slocum saw no reason to deny it. Even if the marshal let him get on the trail of the outlaws, his paint was tuckered out. It seemed every time he had a chance to go after Arnot's gang, his horse was close to dead under him.

Besides, this wasn't even his horse. It belonged to the Butterfield Stagecoach Line.

"I can drive it back," Slocum said.

"You do that, and don't go hittin' too many rocks in the road. That man's worse off than the guard said."

Slocum saw that it was true. The driver's head flopped around like a rag doll's as the deputies shoved him onto the floor of the passenger compartment. The blood oozed steadily from the long track left by the bullet, but head wounds were always dangerous.

Slocum lashed the paint's reins to the rear of the stage, climbed into the box and took the reins. It took him a few minutes to get the team pulling for him and better than ten to get the rig turned around and headed back into Scott's Bluff. The marshal and four deputies flanked him the entire way back.

11

"Ye want a job? Looks like we need a new driver, leastwise fer a week or two. Depends on how fast that stupid sonuvabitch heals." The station agent eyed Slocum closely. "You got a way 'bout ya that keeps men away. Jist what I need drivin' that rig out yonder."

"No, thanks," Slocum said. He couldn't figure how it was the driver's fault that he had been shot by road agents, other than he had been stupid enough to take the job when Arnot's gang worked so openly along northwestern Nebraska roads.

"Gettin' harder 'n hell to get any help. I'll pay double the goin' rate. Twenty bucks a week."

Slocum almost laughed. He could make that much in a single hand of poker, if he found a cowboy drunk enough who didn't know the odds.

"Oh, all right. I'll go thirty. But that's my final offer. Take it or leave it."

"Let's dicker a bit more," Slocum said. Jess got a look in his eye that showed how shrewd the old coot was. Butterfield Stage had chosen well putting him in charge of the Scott's Bluff station.

"What ya wantin'? I'll throw in room 'n board. Thirty, food and a roof o'er yer head."

"You wouldn't need another driver if the stage hadn't been held up," Slocum pointed out. "I'll go after the robbers and stop them. Doesn't look as if the local law's willing to do anything."

"The marshal's jurisdiction don't go that far," Jess said. "Don't blame him. He's got a couple deputies and that's 'bout it. The rest of them what went ridin' to help were all recruited from the saloons."

"I ran across Sheriff Quince, and he seems more inclined to avoid the gang than to run them to ground." Slocum wondered if the sheriff wasn't in cahoots with Arnot.

"Quince ain't sich a bad sort. Plays it close to the vest, if ya know what I mean." Jess took a big chaw of tobacco and worked on it before accurately aiming a gob at the hitching post. "But what he does ain't affectin' what them road agents do. So why should I think you kin stop them owlhoots all by yer lonesome?"

"I'm determined," Slocum said. Jess took a half step back. His eyes widened when he took in the full intensity of Slocum's intent.

"Reckon that makes you them robbers' worst enemy. So you want to git on the Butterfield payroll to stop 'em? Hell, I kin telegraph the home office and get a company of Pinkertons out, if that's what it takes. They're professionals."

"Go on," Slocum said. "Send the telegram. But you know your home office wouldn't send even one Pinkerton. They'd rather continue having their stages held up, thinking this was less expensive than paying for protection. Your drivers and guards are going to go on dying—along with your passengers." Slocum saw that this barb drove deep into the station agent's hide. "You're not getting as many passengers, are you?"

"Preacher man was the first in a week," Jess admitted. "Him and you."

"I don't want to be paid. Give me that paint horse, the gear and a rifle with some ammunition. Supplies for a week or two. I'll do the job for you—for the law."

"That's all?" Jess sounded skeptical. He spat again, this time missing the post by an inch. His gobbet landed in the dusty street and was immediately swallowed by the dryness.

Slocum said nothing. He had endured the marshal's questions and had identified Lawrence and the Dakota Kid's wanted posters, although neither he nor the shotgun guard could identify any of the men who had kidnapped the parson and shot the driver. The marshal had used this lack of positive proof to push aside the notion that Big Ed Lawrence and the Kid were involved. Slocum almost blurted out that he had wounded the Kid in a gunfight but held his tongue.

The way the law worked in this part of Nebraska, he was likely to land in jail again. That seemed to be the favorite way the peace officers operated: throw the witness into a cell for his own protection.

"Ain't likely to need the paint to pull a stagecoach any time soon," Jess said, stroking his stubbled chin. "Won't stand you to more 'n ten dollars worth of supplies, and that includes ammo. You kin use one of the rifles I got inside."

"And?" Slocum heard more in the cagy agent's voice.

"I git half of any reward you collect."

Slocum mentally tallied the rewards he had seen on the posters for Arnot and the others of his gang, including Lawrence and the Dakota Kid. Jess's cut might amount to a thousand dollars, if not more. That was mighty steep for a horse, gear and a few dollars worth of supplies, in addition to Slocum being the one who put his life on the line.

"Done," Slocum said, thrusting out his hand. Jess shook it, then reared back and grabbed a rifle from inside the stage depot's door.

"Here ya go. Git on over to Mckenzie's store and tell him to put whatever you need on the station bill. But no more 'n ten dollars now!"

Slocum wasted no time getting what he needed at the store, slinging it in a pair of burlap bags behind the saddle on the paint. Slocum rode at a steady pace from Scott's

Bluff, not wanting to run into the marshal or any of his deputies, knowing they would do everything in their power to stop him. He doubted they were in cahoots with Arnot, but whatever drove their actions, they might as well be in the outlaw leader's hip pocket. As to Sheriff Quince, Slocum had yet to form a decent opinion. The lawman sounded sincere in wanting to stop the Arnot gang, but Slocum had overheard snippets of conversation that might link the sheriff with the outlaws when he was half-conscious in the Parson's Grove jail cell.

When he was well clear of Scott's Bluff, he slowed and began looking around. This was hilly country that quickly turned mountainous within a dozen miles. That made it perfect for an outlaw's hideout. Tracking would be difficult due to the hard ground and the obscuring bluffs and rust-colored canyons that abounded.

Reaching the spot where the stagecoach had been stopped and the gunfight had ensued, Slocum studied the ground and reconstructed the fight. Spent shotgun shells showed how actively the guard had protected his mail and the lone passenger. Rifle brass gleamed in the afternoon sun, telling Slocum that the attackers had not spared any ammunition as they attacked. The patterns where the piles of brass marked the terrain spoke louder than if he had watched the fight in progress. Two outlaws had come up over a low hill and had laid down a barrage designed to stop any driver. If he had continued along the road, the road agents would have slaughtered his team.

Rather than be a sitting duck for those coming up from either side, the driver had chosen to make a stand. It hadn't lasted long in the hail of bullets Arnot's gang had sent his way.

A single boot heel had crushed grama grass near the road. Slocum doubted it belonged to any of the outlaws or the guard. That meant the preacher man had come from the coach, probably to plead with the outlaws to stop.

Three horses had approached this spot, three had left.

Slocum couldn't tell if one had been riderless on the way in to carry the preacher away. He guessed it had. Sighting along the line of travel gave Slocum a spot to ride toward, a notch in the mountains where a pass might open into an outlaw's hideaway.

He set an easy pace since the sun was going down. He didn't want to reach the pass at twilight when he couldn't see sentries posted in the rocks or along the canyon rims. While it might hide his approach from the outlaws, it worked against him more since he had to enter the sanctuary unseen. Otherwise, Arnot and his men might simply kill Antoinette and their other hostages.

This set off a new line of thinking on Slocum's part. If Arnot was taking men—and women—for ransom, why hadn't there been a hint of a ransom demand? The people of the towns where people vanished pretended the missing had never existed. There was no outrage at exorbitant calls for money. Besides, what kind of money could Arnot hope to get for a baker? Or a preacher?

Were the captives being held as hostage? To what end? Slocum knew there were more questions than answers at the moment. And mostly, he admitted to himself, he didn't care. He would free Antoinette and then worry about the others. If they were even alive.

Slocum shuddered a little at the notion the outlaws were kidnapping people to torture them for their own cruel amusement. The only consolation he had on this score was the baker and how complete the outlaws had been removing his family and all his belongings. They had even taken the baker's dog. Whatever they had in store for the man and his kin, it wasn't likely to be torture if they went to such ends.

The distance to the notch in the towering rock walls turned out to be as deceptive as distances in the desert. The sun dipped low in the west and Slocum had barely covered half the distance. This suited him. He found a ravine, hobbled his paint and then set about fixing dinner. He opened an airtight of beans and used his knife to shovel the gooey contents of the can into his mouth. Lighting a fire would only alert an eager sentry. Slocum doubted Will Arnot posted men who fell down on the job. And if he did, they would nod off only once before going for a dirt nap through all eternity.

He finished his simple meal, buried the airtight and then took his field glasses and scanned the ridge line ahead of him. In less than ten minutes he spotted a small, bright orange spot burning in the night. A slow smile crossed his lips. A sentry was taking a break to roll himself a cigarette and sneak a smoke. Slocum planted a pair of sticks into the hard ground so he could sight along them and study the area at sunup. Then he got his bedroll and flopped down for a good night's sleep. He didn't know when he might get another.

Come morning, he gnawed on a bit of jerky as he went about his preparations. When he was ready to ride, he aligned the two sticks he had thrust into the ground the night before and located where one sentry was likely to be on guard. Using this, Slocum adjusted his approach by going farther to the northeast before cutting back sharply and riding close to the tall, sheer wall of brilliant-hued orange and red rock. Somewhere above him crouched another sentry, looking out toward the prairie but not seeing Slocum. Unless he peered directly over the lip of the canyon rim he would never see anyone directly beneath.

Slocum came to the notch he had ridden toward and studied the ground carefully. Not only did he see evidence of a constant stream of riders in and out, he also spotted what could only be stagecoach tracks. The stages Arnot's gang had stolen were driven this way.

Peering around and looking up into the jagged faces of the canyon walls convinced Slocum he could never simply ride in. There were too many places for a sentry to hide. He had the one spot located where the guard had perched the night before, but nothing betrayed a man's presence there now.

Slocum retreated a ways and found a crevice where he could stake his horse and allow it to eat at sparse grass and even drink from water seeping through the rock and dripping into a small pool. He sat in the mouth of this miniature canyon, thinking hard. There might be other ways into the hideout but it would take weeks to find them. As alert as the sentries appeared, he would be spotted long before he reached Antoinette. That meant he had to enter some other way.

Slocum craned his neck and looked upward. It would be hard, but he could scale the wall and reach the ridge line. He dusted off his hands, then began climbing. The rock was mostly sandstone and gave way under his feet as he tried to scramble up, but he quickly found how to drive the toe of his boot into the rock face and created a step.

An hour after he started, taking rests on ledges on the way up, he finally reached the summit. He had the urge to stand tall and look out across the prairie and the approach to the pass through the mountains. Good sense prevailed, and he flopped onto his belly and lay still while he caught his breath. Standing would silhouette him against the sky.

Slocum was immediately glad he had dropped down because he heard the scrape of boot soles against rock. He lay doggo and waited, not even daring to reach for the six-gun at his hip. With it in a cross-draw holster, he would have to rise up off the ground, unfasten the leather thong over the hammer and then draw. It would betray him to the sentry marching on his route.

Not ten feet away a hat appeared above the edge of a rock. Then the Stetson pushed higher and a face followed. Slocum recognized the face from a wanted poster. He had put it aside because the description had included the indictment of riding with Will Arnot.

The outlaw slipped back out of sight, but Slocum still did not move. Within seconds, the outlaw was back, clambering onto the rock to sit perched there like a lizard basking in the sun. The man took fixings from his pocket and rolled a smoke, lit it and puffed contentedly as he stared out into the distance, alert for any sign of approaching riders.

Slocum knew that if he stared at the man long enough, he would make him uneasy and the outlaw would eventually spot him. But Slocum couldn't take his eyes off the man, fearing detection at any instant. He had to be able to respond instantly if the sentry saw him.

The hot sun arched above and then began to dip, and still Slocum did not move. His feet turned numb from lack of circulation but Slocum vowed to stick it out as long as the sentry sat on the rock, staring ahead. The smallest turn to the side and he would see the intruder.

But Slocum began to realize he was more likely to be seen than to go undetected in spite of the seemingly endless time he had lain motionless. The sentry occasionally stood, stretched his cramped muscles and then fixed another smoke. But he never went to take a leak or leave for a cup of coffee or to get food.

Slocum had to act.

Slowly pushing himself up to hands and knees allowed Slocum to reach under his body for his six-gun. He had it half from the holster when he realized he dared not use it. The report would echo down the canyon pass and to the ears of other sentries. Slocum fastened the six-shooter back in its holster and reached to the top of his boot, drawing his knife. Coming to his knees, he judged distances. Throwing the knife was out of the question—Slocum wasn't good enough to be sure he could kill the outlaw silently. He came to his knees, then rocked to his feet, crouched down and then began a stealthy advance.

He moved like an Indian and never betrayed himself with sound. The sun behind him gave him away. His shadow stretched in front of the guard, who glanced down, then rose and swung his rifle around.

Slocum launched himself and got past the rifle muzzle

to grip the man in a bear hug. With a powerful jerk, Slocum crushed down on the man's back, bending him over and causing him to grunt in pain. The outlaw's rifle dropped to the ground, but he wasn't giving up.

He slammed his forehead into Slocum's face, breaking the grip. Slocum stumbled back, got his balance and brought his knife up, point aimed at the guard's belly.

"Who're you?" the outlaw asked. "You cain't—"

The only reason he asked was to freeze Slocum. The trick didn't work. Slocum launched himself forward but slipped on loose gravel before he could drive the knife home into the road agent's heart. The outlaw grabbed Slocum's wrist and twisted hard. The blade tumbled from Slocum's grasp, forcing him to grapple with the man to keep from being shoved back.

Dropping low, Slocum got his arms around the outlaw's legs. With a powerful upward jerk Slocum upended the man and threw him backward. The man's boots scraped frantically on the rocks as he fought for balance. Then Slocum saw the man wasn't going to make it. On the lip of the sheer drop into the canyon, the man flailed about like a windmill, turned and looked down, then plunged eighty feet to his death.

Slocum dropped to his belly and crept forward, peering over. He had to make sure the outlaw was dead or the rest would come swarming after him. From his vantage point he saw how the man was bent at a curious angle over a boulder. He didn't stir.

Slocum slipped back like a snake slithering through tall grass, retrieved his knife and then inched back to where he had made his way up to the ridge. If his luck held, Arnot would think his sentry had gotten careless and slipped. There was nothing about the corpse to give Slocum away—he was glad he hadn't plugged the man. It'd be hard explaining a bullet hole.

But Slocum found himself facing another dilemma. He had seen firsthand how tight the security was getting into the outlaw hideout. There had to be another way for him to gain entry.

An idea occurred to him as he made his way down the precarious slope, waited for darkness and then rode back to Scott's Bluff.

12

"You been out in the sun too danged long," the station agent said, shaking his head. He took a pull on a bottle of whiskey from the lower drawer, considered offering some to Slocum, then put it back without making the gesture.

"The place is guarded closer than any cavalry outpost," Slocum said. "I can't sneak in, so that means I have to be invited in."

"You could rob the damn bank and see if they'd let you in with the loot."

This startled Slocum. Jess saw the expression on his face and grinned wryly.

"That old fart what runs the bank is worse than the south end of a northbound mule. He charges outrageous interest on loans and is so quick to foreclose he owns half this town. All legal, mind you. He wouldn't have it any other way."

"So you wouldn't mind if I robbed the bank?" Slocum said, amused now.

"Nope. I ain't got no money there."

"But the marshal might not take too kindly to the notion."

"Makes it look more real, you runnin' ahead of a posse intent on stringin' you up."

"The paint you gave me—"

"Loaned you. That piece of horseflesh's Butterfield Stage property."

"The paint that you loaned me isn't up to staying in front of a determined posse. If there was any hesitation on the part of the guards at the mouth of that canyon, I'd be caught in a cross fire. They'd fill me with holes from high up and the marshal and his boys would ventilate me from behind."

"It's yer plan," Jess pointed out.

"Robbing the bank's not part of my plan. I want to make myself so attractive to them that they'll want to kidnap me and take me into their hideout," Slocum said. He had thought long and hard on the subject and decided that Will Arnot was kidnapping people with skills that would be valuable to him. A blacksmith to shoe horses, a doctor to patch up the outlaws if they were wounded, a baker to produce bread to eat—he wasn't sure why they had grabbed Antoinette, but he doubted it was because she was the most beautiful woman this side of the Missouri River. Lawrence and the Kid had been asking after her because of her doctoring skills and were more than a little interested because she was also a schoolteacher.

"If you wore a bag o'er yer head, you couldn't make yerse'f attractive to them," Jess scoffed.

"That's not how I mean. I'll need some more money, but you can have the paint back."

"Now that's right generous of you, givin' me back what's not yers."

Jess complained out of habit, but Slocum saw the man was intrigued by the notion of infiltrating the outlaws' hideout. A little more explanation was all the station agent needed to be pushed over the line into helping Slocum.

"So thass all you want from me?"

"That and money," Slocum said. "I'll get what I need from McKenzie's store and charge it to the stagecoach line, like I did before, and you come on up when I'm ready."

"The marshal'll want to sell you a peddler's license. He charges ten bucks fer somethin' like that."

"Talk to him, tell him I'm doing his job for him, and that he ought to let me sell whatever it is I whup up for a day or two without paying. That'll save you a few dollars."

"Ten dollars," grumbled Jess. "He fines the whores that much a week and you don't want to know what he fines me fer keepin' horses in a corral inside the city limits."

Slocum knew that lawmen made most of their money off petty fines, dead animal removal and serving process. That there weren't any judges with their constables to do the process service meant the marshal got that much more money for his effort. If what Jess said about the banker was right, the marshal might make a tidy sum off foreclosures, too. But the lawman wasn't likely to let one peddler go without ponying up a licensing fee or others would try to sneak by him, no matter the reason.

"I'll get what I need."

"You might check across the street at the saloon, too," Jess said. "The Belgian's been known to put nitric acid in that fancy Peach Fizz drink of his. Ain't never seen a peach floatin' in it, but it has the kick of a mule." Jess wiped his lips, eyes darting toward the desk drawer before returning to business. "You get on with your fixin's. I'll tend to the marshal and ever'thing else."

Slocum left without another word. He knew how the losses weighed on Jess, although the agent tried not to appear worried. More than the loss of a strongbox or mail and even the occasional stage, the outlaws had no compunction against shooting the guard and driver. And Jess had mentioned how slow passenger travel was on the stagecoach line. Nobody in their right mind would dare the trip to Parson's Grove or farther if they worried enough about being kidnapped.

He had to advance his plan carefully without letting any of the townspeople guess what he was up to. As tempting as it was to go the barkeep across the street and ask for a vial of the "special ingredient" for his Peach Fizz, Slocum decided to hunt for other ways of putting a kick into his potion.

He was going to be a patent medicine peddler with elixirs so tempting the outlaws had to kidnap him.

Slocum spent the rest of the day finding discarded pill bottles and other medicine containers, then scouted the countryside for herbs and roots to mix up and put into his witch's brew. It didn't have to do anything other than taste bad. Slocum succeeded in this beyond his wildest expectations. When he tried a nip of the concoction, it almost knocked him off his feet. He had added pure grain alcohol to the roots, coloring and other odds and ends. It burned all the way down his throat, punched him in the belly and then made his head spin.

It was perfect for what he was going to do, and he had mixed a bucket of it.

Item by item, bit by bit, Slocum assembled the rest of his gear. Peddlers didn't wear six-shooters so he spent a few dollars and bought himself a second derringer to hide away. If the outlaws searched him, they'd find one gun but not both. And the knife he left in his boot top. It was both useful and likely to be expected by the outlaws.

After two days of gathering, Slocum went out to an abandoned way station Jess had told him of and began practicing his spiel to the prairie dogs and rabbits. He let his beard grow from a stubble to a fair length, then carefully trimmed it into a goatee and mustache guaranteed to keep people from recognizing him as the same man who had thundered through town a week before, if they didn't study him too carefully. He finished his disguise with a long black cutaway coat, violet-tinted rectangular glasses and a battered bowler he found blowing along out on the prairie.

When he got restless enough he contacted Jess and told him he was ready. Packing his valise with the vials of Doctor Jackson's Miraculous All-Healing Potion, he waited for the stage to rumble up. Jess had telegraphed that there would be a new passenger getting on.

He had been John Slocum when he went to the way station. Now he was Doctor Phineas Jackson.

He rode into town and immediately began haranguing anyone who would even slow to look at him. And eventually, giving Jess a discreet sign, he went to the stage built at the end of town for political speeches and hangings, put up his signs and walked to the front center of the stage. Slocum felt a momentary giddiness as people began assembling. Anything that robbed them of their dreary routine was noteworthy.

He had never been the center of attention like this before. He cleared his throat, pretended this was the war and all the people were his troops awaiting his orders. From there it went easier. He rolled into his encomium, promising results only a trifle short of eternal life for his potion.

"What's it cure 'sides warts? Ain't got no warts," Jess called out on cue.

"It'll cure warts, yes," Slocum said, "but it will also cure your gray hair. Try some, sir." Slocum tossed a bottle down to Jess, who fielded it. When he pulled the cork and sniffed, he recoiled but tried to stifle the reaction. He glared up at Slocum, then took a healthy swig. Jess paused, then took another and wobbled a mite on his feet.

"Don't see that it's curin' Jess of gray hair none," one man said.

"It's workin'. I feel it!" Jess cried, his voice hoarse from the potion.

Slocum tossed him down a towel, and Jess ran it through his hair, then carefully discarded the towel, leaving behind hair that was noticeably less white than before. No one noticed the flour on the towel he had discarded or that Jess had liberally applied bootblack to his hair before dusting it with flour.

"It worked! Jess got rid of his white hair!" Slocum called. "And it'll grow hair on your egg-bald knobs, too!"

He launched into an improbable list of things it would do, but he waited and finally got the next shill—this one hired by Jess.

"Mister," came a piteous call from a young boy, "I got a real bad pain in my gut. The doc said it was somethin' inside eatin' me alive. I'm gonna die."

Slocum beckoned the boy closer. As the youngster neared, Slocum saw Big Ed Lawrence at the back of the crowd, standing on tiptoe, trying to get a better look. Slocum made sure he kept his back turned to the outlaw as he opened a vial and handed it to the boy.

"Just a drop or two, no more. You've got serious problems, but this is serious medicine."

The boy drank more than Slocum had said, his eyes going wide and out of focus for a moment, then he turned toward the crowd, grabbed his stomach and doubled over.

"I feel, I feel *sick!*" the boy cried. A torrent of blood and chicken parts that had been concealed in a small bag looked as if they spewed from his mouth. The crowd gasped and took a step back. Complete silence fell then.

Then the boy straightened and wiped his mouth.

"I , , , I feel all cured. I ain't got no pain no more. You cured me, Doctor Jackson!"

"My secret potion cured you, son," Slocum said solemnly. He saw that Lawrence had turned and quickly mounted his horse. He galloped from town. Slocum had found the right combination of pitch and blarney to interest the outlaws.

"I need two bottles. Make it three!" cried a man Slocum had not planted in the crowd. He felt a tad of guilt selling the worthless concoction—but not much. They might suffer from a bellyache or even get drunk, but it was for a good cause. It was to rescue Antoinette and others taken by the Arnot gang.

When he had sold his entire valise full of bottles, Slocum chased the crowd away. A few tried to make him promise to manufacture more for their ailments. He skirted answering the best he could.

At the stagecoach depot a while later, Jess sat behind his

desk and the youngster was perched on a chair across the room. Slocum dropped the wad of money he had taken from the crowd for the bogus elixir.

"Good performance," Slocum told the urchin.

"Done it before. How much you payin' me?" The boy looked at Jess, not at Slocum.

"Like we 'greed upon. Five dollars."

"Five! I whupped up fifty dollars o' business!"

"Six," Jess dickered. They finally came to an agreement at eight. The boy grabbed the money and was gone so fast Slocum thought a tornado blew through.

"And the rest goes back into the company strongbox, it bein' what I done advanced ya," Jess said. Slocum doubted a dime of it would be returned to the Butterfield coffers, and he didn't care. Lawrence had taken the bait. With any luck, the next stage from Scott's Bluff would be held up.

And he would be kidnapped for the secret to his fabulous curative.

"Stage'll be rumblin' in 'bout any time now," Jess said. He squinted at Slocum. "You surely do look the part of a medicine peddler. But you got a gun?"

"Don't worry. I can always throw some of that elixir on them," Slocum said.

"Kinder to jist shoot the sonsabitches." Jess cocked his head to one side and then jerked his thumb over his shoulder. "There's the stage, only an hour late."

"Where's it heading?" Slocum asked.

"Don't matter to you none," Jess said. "I got yer trunk all ready to load on."

Slocum felt a pang of nervousness that quickly settled into a coldness. He was on the verge of paying back the outlaws for everything they had done—and rescuing Antoinette. He felt it in his bones. The driver braked hard and jumped to the ground, worked to change teams and them clambered back into the box to look down at Slocum.

"Git yer ass in, mister. We got time to make up."

"It's Doctor Jackson," Slocum said haughtily. He noticed two hard cases lounging nearby who watched with particular interest and figured they were part of Arnot's gang. "I make the best—"

"Git in or git left," the driver snapped.

Slocum climbed in and slammed the door behind him. He was the only passenger, as he had hoped. Jess hadn't twisted too many schedules to leave him the only passenger. Folks weren't travelling the way they had.

The stagecoach lurched and threw Slocum back hard against the seat, then took a quick turn and hit the road and every pothole. From the direction the coach was heading, Slocum decided they were going to Parson's Grove. That suited him fine. If the outlaws didn't take the bait, he could retrieve his Indian pony and work on some other scheme.

He was so intent on running over what he would do when the outlaws attacked that he hardly noticed the driver begin to slow, but he did take note when he glanced over and saw a sawed-off shotgun poking through the stagecoach window. A masked man trotted alongside, the scattergun pointed directly at Slocum's face.

"Whoa, mister, don't go shootin'. I got some fine medicines, but nothing that'd fix a dozen double-ought buckshot holes in my chest."

The stage rattled to a halt and the outlaw yanked open the door.

"Out," he ordered.

"But I have no money. Well, a little," Slocum said, trying to keep in character. He peered at the road agent through his violet-tinted spectacles. In the setting sun, the man almost disappeared.

"Got his gear?" the outlaw called to a pair of others.

"Got it," they confirmed.

"You can have my medicine. Take it all. I'll even give you my secret formula. And what money I have. Here, take this," Slocum said, holding out a few greenbacks. The outlaw snatched the scrip from his hand and threw it high into the air so the wind caught it. The bills fluttered about on the sluggish breeze and then came down, impaled on the sharp spines of a clump of prickly pear cactus.

Slocum protested for show, then he fought for real when the two outlaws behind him grabbed him and pulled a bag over his head. He was completely blind inside the black cloth sack.

"Get him into the wagon. We won't make it tonight but will by dawn."

Louder, so the driver could hear, the outlaw shouted, "Move your no-account ass. Next time, we'll take the rig— and your life!"

The driver muttered curses, then snapped the reins and got the frightened team pulling. Slocum heard the stage racing down the road toward Parson's Grove and almost wished he were still on it. The men roughly shoved him from side to side and then spun him around several times to disorient him, then they threw him like a sack of potatoes into the rear of a buckboard.

"Stay down and if you try to peek out of that blindfold, you're a dead man."

Slocum leaned back and tried to enjoy the bone-jarring ride, gleeful that his plan had worked so well up to this point. After what he estimated to be an hour of travel, they drew rein and camped for the night, then were up and on the trail again as the sun warmed the outside of the black bag Slocum wore. He was getting a mite antsy not taking off the bag all through the night, but he gritted his teeth and endured increasingly rough roads.

It occurred to him that they were probably in the canyon he had failed to penetrate before. And they had passed the point where the guard had fallen to his death. Slocum vowed more of the outlaws would follow that one to hell when the buckboard creaked and swayed and came to a halt.

"We're here," the leader said. He yanked off the bag. The bright sunlight momentarily blinded Slocum. Then he saw the valley ringed in by towering mountains, some still capped with snow in spite of the lateness in summer. Twisting about, the only way out of the valley was directly behind, through the canyon pass he knew was well guarded.

The town set like a jewel in a green crown in the middle of a meadow. This was no ordinary outlaw hideout. This was a prosperous, well-built town that would be the envy of any in the region with twice the population. Houses were separated by picket fences and the streets were well kept, with none of the rocks and holes he associated with Scott's Bluff and other Nebraska towns. Most impressive was the large three-story building in the middle of the town. Slocum had seen army forts that were less well built. And everywhere he looked, men and women went about their business, laughing and enjoying themselves. No one appeared to be held against their will.

"Welcome to Refugio," the outlaw said, laughing harshly. "It's gonna be your home—forever."

13

The outlaws started to leave him where he stood. Slocum was taken aback by this. He was their prisoner, but they weren't treating him like one.

"What am I supposed to do?"

"Git yer gear over at the receiving depot," said one of the outlaws. "Then you gotta stay alive like everyone else."

"How?"

The outlaws exchanged looks and then shook their heads before leaving him in the dust. Slocum watched the buckboard rattle away and followed it, not sure where else to go. A glance behind him convinced Slocum that returning through the narrow canyon wasn't likely to do him any good. Besides, he had gone to considerable trouble to come to Refugio.

Refugio. The name rolled over and over in his head. A refuge. A place for outlaws of all stripe to come, to hide, to lie low until the law no longer actively sought them. It made sense, but Slocum wondered about the majority of the men and women he saw as he trooped through the middle of the town.

The street was broad and lacking in potholes like most western towns. The buildings were in good repair, too. Some were brick but many were wood planking, telling him the Arnot gang had a forest somewhere near to pillage for timber. He saw a half dozen men actively working to paint a new store. He slowed and saw the sign going up.

"Hey," Slocum called. "Is that going to be the bakery?"

"Cain't read, eh?" An old man with a crippled leg hobbled around and stared at the sign being constructed. "Yep. We finally got ourselves a decent baker. I can almost smell the bread bakin' now." The old man scowled as he looked Slocum over. He spat, wiped his mouth and said, "You ain't the new baker. I seen him. But you're new to Refugio. Ain't seen you here before."

"I just got into town," Slocum said sardonically.

"Figured that. What's your speciality?"

"Beg your pardon?" Slocum pushed his violet-tinted glasses back up his nose and stared at the old man. He wore a six-shooter slung low on his hip. A quick glance at the other workers showed none of them wore sidearms. And around town most of the townspeople went unarmed, but dotted throughout the crowd were a few men with six-shooters. Slocum began to get a better notion of how things were done in Refugio.

"Why'd they bring you here?"

"I concoct fine patent medicines," Slocum said. "They can cure what ails you."

"Ain't nothin' ailin' me," the old man said brusquely.

"Might be able to fix up that gimpy leg of yours. A dose or two of—"

"I'd never let a quack like you within a country mile of my leg. No sir, not when we got ourselves a purty new doctor."

Slocum's ears pricked up at this. It could only be Antoinette Thibadeaux.

"I work good with medical doctors. Where can I find this newcomer of yours?"

"Don't even think of it, mister," the old man said, resting his hand on the butt of his six-gun. "She's got special protection, especially from the likes of you. We've had bad luck with our doctors, and this time Refugio's gonna hang onto her. The womenfolk especially have taken a liking to her."

"I can furnish actual medicines, more than the patent medicines I sell," Slocum said.

"Look around town. You'll find the doctor's office," the old man said.

"It's allowed?"

The old man laughed harshly.

"Everything's allowed, 'cept you leavin'. You're here for the rest of your miserable life, so you might as well enjoy it."

"Reckon I could with some fresh bread."

"Then go sell some of your quack potions, get some money and buy it. He'll be workin' into the night to fix the first batch for dawn tomorrow. Took us nigh on forever to get an oven built to suit him. About time he earned his keep."

With that the old man bellowed at his painters, got them working harder and left Slocum wondering at the grip Will Arnot had on this town. The men with guns were undoubtedly his trusted gang. But there were quite a few of them. Almost too many for Slocum to believe Arnot commanded each and every one.

He continued on his way and stopped at what looked like a railroad depot except there were no railroad tracks coming into the station.

"What kin I do you out of, mister?" The man in the ticket agent's cage peered out at him.

"A ticket out of Refugio," Slocum said, wondering what the reply might be.

"You ain't got enough money, and you never will." The agent reached down, fumbled a second, then placed a six-shooter on the sill in front of him. This was as clear an indication that he was one of Arnot's gang as anything.

"The road agents who brought me here said I could get my gear."

"Oh, you're the snake oil salesman. Sure thing. Go on around back. Up on the platform in a stack. Some of it's bound to be yours. Take only your stuff. We don't cotton much to thieves around here." The agent lifted his pistol, aimed it at Slocum, then slowly diverted the barrel until he pointed down the street to where the three-story citadel loomed. For the first time Slocum saw the gallows beside it. The huge structure dwarfed everything else around it, including the platform with the noose slowly swinging in the wind.

"Whatever you do, don't go crossin' anybody who can send you to the hangman," the agent said in a friendly voice. "The last three hangin's been something of a fiasco. Two of 'em choked to death and the third's head popped right on off. Sounded like the cork blowing out of a champagne bottle, it did."

Slocum had the feeling hangings were part of Refugio's recreation. Or Arnot's.

"Where do I find the fellow in charge of all this?"

"You mean the mayor?"

"If he's the one who runs things." Slocum hesitated to name Will Arnot outright since he didn't want to draw too much attention to himself, not after he had worked so hard to get here in one piece. He knew Antoinette was also in the town, as well as the baker who had been kidnapped from Parson's Grove. He suspected others who had mysteriously vanished were similarly employed around town.

"You don't want to see him. Ever. He's bad medicine, and the only time he shows his ugly face is to snap at somebody."

"What about the . . . marshal?"

Slocum thought this would produce a gale of laughter. A lawman in a town of outlaws seemed outrageous, but he got a somber reply.

"The marshal's around somewhere. Always is. Keepin' the peace in Refugio is harder 'n you'd think." The agent moved his six-gun off the shelf and tucked it away out of sight again. "Not many laws here, but the one that gets you in hot water the fastest is tryin' to escape. Don't even think of it. Some of the boys are in Will Arnot's gang and the rest are just campin' out here, payin' for the privilege to keep from bein' . . . annoyed. You catch my drift?"

Slocum nodded.

"I'll fetch my belongings after I've finished looking around. Where's a good place to stay?"

"You kin sleep under the platform out back, least until you get some money."

"How do you know I don't have any money?" asked Slocum. This produced the laughter he had expected earlier.

"Nobody what gets brung to Refugio has a dime in his pocket. We're a bunch of thieves, mister. *Thieves*. That's why we're all here, and that's why you're here. We're hidin' out but you been vanished."

"And you're hiding out," Slocum guessed.

"Don't talk about it in town. Lot of mighty nervy gents here."

Slocum's hand went to his hip, but he touched only slick cloth. He hadn't dared hide his trusty Colt Navy in his gear and had relied on the two derringers, of which one was taken during the search the outlaws had made back on the road. He was glad he had decided to bring a second and put it where he might not be able to draw it fast but would still have it unless they tore apart his boots.

Walking around the depot showed where several mounds of gear had been piled. Slocum poked through his, found a few bottles of the witch's brew he had conjured up and tucked them into his voluminous coat pocket. He might as well try to sell some to get money while he cased the town. The three-story structure next to the gallows drew him like a lodestone draws iron.

He approached slowly, taking in the details slowly rather than greedily examining the large fort in the center of town. Where most towns might have a gazebo for band concerts or the Spanish-settled areas a plaza, a twenty-foot square blockhouse dominated Refugio. At the top of the thirty foot walls he saw loops cut for riflemen to peer out and shoot anyone coming. Properly provisioned, this small fort could hold off an entire troop of cavalry for quite a while.

Which might be the reason it had such thick walls and barred entry points. He saw two doors, both on the same wall and both heavily protected. A single rifleman on the walkway above could keep anyone from entering either of the portals, both of which were wide enough to move in ample supplies. As Slocum stood studying the layout, a loud voice called down to him from above.

"You, keep moving. No gawking. Ain't allowed."

Slocum looked up and saw the sentry on the wall pointing a large bore rifle at him, possibly a Sharps .50 buffalo gun. Not only did the outlaws command the height in the center of the verdant valley, they also had the firepower to reach out a considerable ways if all their guards had such powerful rifles. Slocum didn't doubt for an instant that the sentry was marksman enough to hit what he aimed at, either.

"Sorry, new in town," Slocum called. He started to go, then halted. In keeping with his disguise, he called back, "You need a potion for your aches and pains? Got a good deal on a bottle of Professor Jones's Magical Tonic." Slocum struggled to remember what he had called the vile concoction back in Parson's Grove. Since there hadn't been any printed labels, it didn't matter—and Slocum doubted the guard was likely to be able to read, even if there had been some evidence he had mixed up the name.

"Got a back twinge now and again," the guard shouted down. "That stuff any good for back pain?"

"You are in luck, sir! The first use of my fabulous tonic was for back pain."

"How much?"

"A single dollar will buy relief," Slocum said, shifting his gaze from the sentry to the barred portals. It'd be worth a dollar to get a look inside and here the guard was going to pay him for the bottle of worthless medicine and let him look around for nothing.

"You stay right where you are," the guard said. Slocum moved a bit to the side so he could get a good look when the barred door swung wide.

But it didn't swing open. A small opening, hardly large enough for Slocum to see the guard's face, opened beside the locked entry. The guard shoved his ugly face out far enough so Slocum could see him.

"Get your ass over here so you can give me the potion. My back's twinging up something fierce right now."

Slocum walked slowly, trying to look around the man's head. All he saw were shadows inside. Whether another guard was inside, Slocum couldn't tell.

"Here you are. One dollar." Slocum held it up.

"Pass it inside."

"Money first. No way I could ever collect with you holed up in such a strong fortress," Slocum said, trying to draw out the man.

"Be like that. Here." The guard flung a silver dollar out, and Slocum snared it easily.

"You trust me to give you the potion?" Slocum asked.

"Of course I do. We got a mountain howitzer in here, and I'll use it on you. Ever seen what one of them things can do to a human body, loaded with chain?"

"It sounds mighty dangerous," Slocum said going to the peephole and holding up the bottle of liquid.

"We got enough to hold off an army for a month. Longer! Now gimme."

Slocum handed the guard the bottle. The sentry popped the cork and took a long pull. He belched, wiped his lips and asked, "You got another of these? My back's feeling better by the minute."

Since the main ingredient of Slocum's patent medicine was alcohol, there was hardly any miracle being wrought. He silently passed another bottle and received a second silver cartwheel in payment. As the guard stepped away to sample this bottle, Slocum got a better look behind the man. A lone lantern cast wan light across crates all marked with U.S. ARMY on the sides. Slocum had enough experience to know these were stolen rifles. He didn't see the mountain howitzer the guard had bragged on but didn't doubt its existence for an instant. Another pile beyond the rifles looked to be food.

"You might want to cut the dose with some water, if that's too strong for you," Slocum said. "You want me to fetch some water?"

"Got all we need in here from a pump," the guard said. "Thanks. And if you got more of this, maybe you can bring it by later. Around midnight."

"That I will," Slocum said. He had learned how difficult it would be to pry loose anyone in that fortress. They had rifles, undoubtedly enough ammo to feed them, supplies for a month and possibly a well to furnish water. Will Arnot had built himself a first-class hideout.

Slocum decided it was high time that he saw the outlaw leader and had a few words with him.

Taking his time walking back down the street away from the citadel, Slocum took in every detail he could. The longer he walked, the more he marvelled at the cleanliness and order in town. The people waved to one another, though not to him, and appeared friendly enough. But the lack of iron on most of the men's hips told Slocum this wasn't the carefree town it appeared on the surface. The few men strutting about with six-shooters prominently displayed were given wide berth by those who didn't pack.

He stopped in front of the saloon and looked inside. A taste of whiskey would be good right about now, and he knew this was the one spot in town where loose tongues flapped freely and men said things they might not otherwise. But as he stepped through the double doors, two armed men came up to him, one on either side.

"You're new in town," said the rangy man on his left. It wasn't a question.

"Reckon so, and getting here has built quite a thirst."

"You can't come in here," said the other one, a stockier man with a nervous tic under his left eye. His hand twitched occasionally, as if only force of will kept him from drawing his six-gun and killing Slocum on the spot.

Slocum looked around and saw that all the men inside the saloon wore pistols. They were all part of Arnot's gang—or were paying the gang leader enough to hang out here so they wouldn't get hanged outside the protective mountains surrounding this hideout.

"Didn't know," Slocum said, backing out of the saloon. The two men followed to be sure he went on his way. As Slocum walked the rest of the way down the main street, he saw how forced the smiles of the rest of the citizens were and how they stared with not a little bit of fear and hatred at those carrying six-shooters.

Slocum considered his options as he sauntered along, trying to look unconcerned. He saw how the two outlaws from the saloon dogged him now, one on each side of the street. Slocum knew better than to seek out Antoinette now so he turned into the blacksmith, intending to use his patent medicine selling as a cover to see how and where the outlaws corralled their horses. Without a fast horse, Slocum doubted it would be possible to escape this tidy little prison.

"Afternoon," Slocum greeted. The smithy looked up and grunted, then went back to stoking his fire until it was red-hot. He took a pair of pincers, grabbed a partly formed horseshoe and began heating it in his forge.

"A man like you must get his share of aches and pains," Slocum said, looking around. He didn't see where any horse was tethered, waiting for the horseshoe to be completed. "I've got just the thing for your pain."

"Get out of here. You ain't one of them."

The venom in the blacksmith's voice put Slocum on guard.

"Them?"

"The road agents, the sonsabitches who kidnapped me and brought me here." The smithy swung his hammer and almost flattened the piece of iron he heated.

"I'm like you," Slocum said. "They brought me here. I sell medicine."

"You ain't like me and if you don't get out of here, they'll kill you."

"You're wrong," Slocum said. "We're both in the same predicament."

"Like hell." The smithy moved away from the forge. Slocum saw the man's left leg had been amputated. In its place was a wooden peg. His right leg was twisted and bent and held straight by an elaborate iron frame.

"I made it myself after they busted up my legs so I couldn't try getting away—again." The smithy tapped the iron apparatus. "They said the next one I'd need to make would be for my neck, if I didn't do what they said."

"You were the smithy in Agate, weren't you? Billy Benbow's your name?"

The flash of fear on the man's face was enough to tell Slocum he had scored a bull's-eye.

"My friends in Agate never came lookin' for me," the smithy said. "Probably for the best. I had friends there, friends who'd work real hard and good for these miserable sidewinders. Don't want that. And I don't want no more trouble. Get out of here. Nobody but me and them's allowed here." The way Benbow spoke so bitterly, Slocum guessed Arnot kept a close watch on anyone poking about, asking about horses or other ways out of Refugio. And there was something else. If any man in town was capable of making weapons to use against the outlaws, it would be the blacksmith.

"Here," Slocum said, putting a bottle of his patent medicine on a table. "On the house."

"Thanks," the smithy said, eyeing it. He, like the guard at the blockhouse, knew the fake medicine was probably more alcohol than anything else. From what Slocum had experienced back at the saloon, only the outlaws were allowed to drink. That made his patent medicine all the more valuable.

Slocum left the sweltering blacksmith's shop and took a deep breath. The indescribable odor of baking bread made his mouth water. He followed the aroma back down the street to the store where the workmen had finished their repair work. The baker was inside the store, kneading another batch of dough for his ovens.

Slocum went inside. If he was going to find an ally getting out of Refugio, it had to be the baker. He knew the man was almost as recently arrived as he was and wouldn't have settled into the routine—and fear—of captivity yet.

The baker looked up when Slocum came in.

"Can't sell you any. First batch goes to Arnot."

Slocum nodded. This was an interesting tidbit of information.

"Need a deliveryman?"

"Get out of here," the baker said. He was short, rotund and had wide-spaced brown eyes. Streaks of flour painted him up like an Indian on the warpath. He wiped his hands on his apron, but this did nothing to remove the sticky dough clinging to his fingers. "Out!"

"I was in the hotel when I saw them kidnap you," Slocum said. "We can get out of Refugio, but we're going to have to work together."

"You don't understand. They have my family. It . . . it's as if I am stuck here forever. If I try to get away, they'll kill my wife and daughter.

"And your dog," Slocum said. The instant he said it, he saw stark fear cross the baker's face. He turned as pale as the flour streaking his forehead and cheeks.

"You're one of them. You're trying to see if I'm planning anything. I'm not. I'm staying!"

"I went to your house and saw evidence how they had removed everything, including your dog," Slocum said, but he knew he had made a bad mistake. The baker put the preparation table between them and continued to edge away.

"I haven't seen you around here before. Or in town. Where I used to live." The baker was almost stammering now.

"I want to help. You and your family."

"Help!" the baker shouted. He dashed around the table and burst into the street yelling at the top of his lungs.

Before Slocum could quiet him down, the two outlaws from the saloon appeared like ghosts out of the twilight. The one with the nervous twitch drew his six-shooter in a smooth, lightning-fast movement and ran for the front door of the bakery.

Slocum knew better than to stay. He had no idea what the penalty for even talking about escaping Refugio was, but the memory of the gallows refused to go away.

Darting out the back door, Slocum looked around for somewhere to hide. He didn't see anywhere—and the two outlaws were already coming through the bakery, their boots crashing heavily on the wood floor as they ran to capture him.

14

If he ran, he would be a sitting duck. There was nowhere to hide and the open stretch from the back of the bakery made it impossible to reach any hiding spot fast enough to matter. Slocum turned and saw that the painters had left a ladder propped against the side of the building. In a move of desperation, Slocum leaped to the ladder and clambered up the rungs as fast as he could. Before he reached the top and the dubious safety of the roof, the two gunmen burst out, alert for the shot that would rob Slocum of his life.

He clung to the sides of the ladder, pulse hammering. Slocum wondered if they could hear his pounding heart or smell the sweat beading on his forehead. In the dim light, they almost vanished because of the violet tint to his glasses. He wanted to toss aside those glasses to get a better look at the pair but dared not move. More than this, Slocum had always been aware that staring at someone would draw attention—but he couldn't take his eyes off the gunmen.

"Where'd the varmint go?" asked the stocky, nervous one.

The taller one slowly surveyed the land behind the bakery, not missing a detail. He stepped out and looked left and right. Slocum waited for him to see the ladder and look up. All the outlaw had to do then was squeeze off an easy shot and end it.

A sudden noise inside the bakery caused both men to whirl about.

"What's going on in there?" demanded the rangier outlaw.

"We musta missed him. He hid out and that's him gettin' away. Willie's gonna skin us alive if we let him escape."

"Skin us? He'll do a hell of a lot worse. He'll have us swingin' from a rope rather than that damned snake oil salesman."

The men crowded back into the bakery, giving Slocum the chance to complete his climb. He moved as softly as he could. Any sound against the shingled roof would echo below and give him away. But gunshots rang out, filled the bakery and then spilled into the street beyond. From his vantage point, Slocum saw a dozen armed men racing toward the bakery. If they took up the hunt, his goose would be cooked for sure.

"What's going on?" demanded a lumbering man swinging a shotgun from side to side as he huffed and puffed up.

"The baker. He tried to jump us," said the nervous one of the outlaw pair. "We didn't have no choice but to plug him."

"Damnation, and him with only one batch of bread baked. The boss is not going to like this, no sir. We snatched that baker fellow because he was so good."

"Best in Nebraska," piped up another. "I know. I sampled his bread a half dozen times before Arnot believed he was as good as I said."

"You got a fat head as well as a fat gut, Roy," snapped the man with the shotgun. As the large man turned, Slocum caught the glint of light off a badge pinned to the man's vest. He doubted the laws being enforced were those of most towns. What Will Arnot wanted was his law, not a code carefully written to furnish any protection for the citizens of Refugio.

"Why'd the baker go loco on you?" asked the one named Roy. "You upped and shot him, but he was all broke, as far as his spirit went. I oughta know. I was the one who brung him and his family in."

"The patent medicine peddler was making noises about escaping town," said the taller of the men below. "We had to stop him."

"He got plumb away," said the nervous gunman. "We better find him. He talked to the blacksmith about a horse, and he was tryin' to recruit the baker in some cockamamie escape plan."

Slocum knew the twitchy outlaw was making this up, but it was a good guess. Too close for comfort.

"Where's he gonna go? He just got to Refugio. He don't know anybody. Even if he did, nobody's dumb enough to go along with a plan." The stocky fake lawman thumped the barrel of his shotgun against his left palm, as if wanting to use it as a club rather than shotgun.

"I'll put somebody to watchin' his pile of shit over at the depot," said the rangy outlaw. "Gustav ought to earn his pay, sittin' on his cracker ass all day pretendin' to be a ticket agent."

Slocum reckoned Gustav was the man he had spoken to after arriving in Refugio. From the way the man had acted, he doubted he could ever convince him to go along with an escape—and Gustav had shown him a six-gun, a symbol of which side of authority he was on in town. He was Arnot's man, through and through.

"I don't like the way he just upped and disappeared," the twitchy gunman said. He looked around. Slocum froze. Any movement might draw unwanted attention. But the outlaw's attention quickly changed to a fight in front of the saloon where he must be a bouncer. He, the taller outlaw and the marshal lit out at a run to put an end to the fistfight before it escalated into gunplay.

Slocum might cling to the roof all night and be caught eventually or he could act now, while the fight distracted the outlaws. He let loose, slid to the edge of the roof, then wiggled over the verge. He hung by his fingertips for an instant, then dropped as quietly as possible to the ground. He rounded the bakery and stayed in shadow as he made his way toward the far end of town. He had not been this way and had not found Antoinette. It stood to reason the doctor's office was in this direction.

If it wasn't, Slocum knew he was in deep trouble.

Flitting like a ghost, he worked away from the brighter lights in the middle of Refugio and finally spotted a solitary building off by itself. The light in the rear window cast enough illumination for him to see a doctor's shingle swinging slowly in the gentle night wind. He couldn't read the name but guessed this had to be where Antoinette had set up her practice.

Bent double, Slocum made his way to the window and chanced a look inside. A small, neat, empty bedroom disappointed him. He had expected to see Antoinette.

Slocum froze in his tracks when he heard a six-gun cock behind him.

"I'll shoot you in the back, if I have to," came the low voice. "Don't make me."

"I'd rather you let me turn around so we could face each other," Slocum said. "I'm a sight prettier to look at straight on."

"John!"

As Slocum turned he found himself almost bowled over as the woman jumped into the air, threw her arms around his neck and tried to smother him with kisses. Her weight unbalanced him enough to stagger back and crash into the wall.

"I worried you'd never find me. How'd you do it? How are we going to get out of here?" Antoinette reared back enough to give him a good look. "You let your beard grow. And you have a mustache. And you've changed your clothes."

"I do that from time to time," Slocum said, his arm around her waist to hold her close. "Sometimes, I even take a bath."

"Not recently," Antoinette said, her pert nose wrinkling in mock disapproval.

"Let's get inside. I have some hard cases looking for me."

"You don't have a gun," she said, her hands running down his hips. "That means you're not one of them. I mean, they don't think you're an outlaw."

"They kidnapped me, just as they did you."

"And poor Doc Zacharias. They brought him here, but he tried to escape once too often. They hanged him as an example for everyone else."

"And then they didn't have a doctor, so they 'vanished' you," Slocum said. "I reckon Zacharias was lucky, though."

"Lucky? How can you say that?" Antoinette was outraged.

He told her he had found Billy Benbow and what the outlaws had done to keep him in town.

"I didn't know. I liked Billy." Antoinette turned away from Slocum. "Truth to tell, I was sweet on him, but he never gave me a second glance."

"More than his legs are bent and broken, then," Slocum said. He closed the door behind her. They stood in the outer office of the surgery. To one side stood a large desk. On the other side was a low table with a sheet on it—the examination table.

"I know something that's not bent at all," Antoinette said, her hand slipping down the front of Slocum's shirt and then moving lower. "Is this the right time?"

"Seems to be," Slocum said. Getting out of Refugio might be impossible, and they'd both end up in unmarked graves if they tried to escape now. Taking the time now was both a reward for getting into Refugio and an incentive for getting out with Antoinette.

"Well, sir, we have to do this right. Since Dr. Zacharias is no longer here—"

"Good," Slocum said, kissing her ear before moving lower on her swanlike throat.

"Then I must do everything like a doctor would."

"Not like Zacharias, I hope," Slocum said, moving still lower and beginning to pop free the buttons on her blouse to reveal the milky swells of her breasts.

"No, not like him. No, oh, yes, John, there! Oh!"

Slocum barely got his arms around the woman's trim waist as her legs gave way. He had worked his tongue under her blouse and found the hardened point capping one breast. He had sucked the nub into his mouth and ran his tongue over it briskly, causing Antoinette's reaction. He swept her up and spun her around, sitting her on the examination table, her legs dangling over the edge.

"Who's doing the examining?" she asked, her breath coming in harsh pants. She was flushed. Slocum saw the flood of crimson spread from her cheeks to her throat and lower to her chest. He teased and tormented with his mouth, sucking one mound of flesh into his mouth, then pushing it away slowly with his tongue before moving to the other.

Antoinette collapsed backward onto the table. Slocum lost his oral contact, then decided on more exciting areas of exploration. He reached down and pulled up her skirts until they bunched around her waist. She wasn't wearing any undergarments, leaving her naked, exposed.

"Go on, do it, John. Oh, oh, yes, ohhh!"

Antoinette's body shivered as if she had a fever when he gently parted her legs and buried his face in the fragrant, tangled nest he found between those firm, white thighs. His tongue lapped and licked delicate flesh before dipping into the salty well of her being. Every time he dragged his lips across her nether lips, she trembled a bit more, and when he kissed the tiny pink bud that had popped up at the upper end of her fleshy portals, she lifted her hips from the table and tried to cram herself into his face. Slocum continued his avid oral ministrations as passions hidden within the woman were unleashed like a prairie tornado.

When they died down and her legs limply dropped on either side of his body, he knew he wasn't able to hold back his own desires any longer. Reaching down he unfastened his fly and let the log-thick shaft bounce out.

Antoinette propped herself up on her elbows and peered at him in the dim light. Her eyes widened, and she licked her lips in anticipation.

"I thought we were through, but we're just getting started. That looks so scrumptious!" She sat up and reached for him, guiding him inward until the rubbery tip of his manhood brushed across the area he had lavished with his kisses minutes before.

A new temblor of delight racked the woman, and she fell back flat on the table. Slocum reached under her knees and hiked her feet up to the table, then spread her legs wide as he moved forward. They both gasped as he penetrated her. For a moment, Slocum simply stood, hands on the woman's trembling legs, surrounded by her clinging, warm, moist flesh. Then he could not restrain himself. He began stroking powerfully, moving to and fro with need. The heat mounted along the length of his manhood until he was sure he was going to char himself to a stump.

Antoinette's urgings, her soft moans, her loud cries of pleasure, drove him on. Slocum moved faster. Every stroke was full-bore, as deep and hard as he could make them. She began writhing about and crying out in passion. Antoinette gripped the edges of the examination table to keep from sliding. More than this she pulled herself toward him with every inward thrust.

They strove together, Slocum sure that he would never be able to continue past the next stroke. The stark desires burned within him, but his need to make this last kept him from spilling his seed like a young buck. He bent forward, then rocked his hips inward fast, only to withdraw slowly. But even his determination to make such delight last all night faded as animal needs overwhelmed him.

Crying out lustily, he sank his balls deep and exploded. Antoinette gasped and then a new earthquake of released lust shook her body.

Spent, Slocum sagged forward, his cheek resting against Antoinette's breasts. She stroked his hair for a moment, then pushed him away and sat up.

"What's that? John! Outside!"

Slocum was already moving. He hastily fastened his fly and looked around for a weapon. Retrieving the derringer he had concealed in his boot would take too long if Arnot's men broke in.

"Who's there?" called Antoinette, motioning for Slocum to hide behind the examination table. He crouched down, waiting to see what was required.

"You all right?"

Slocum recognized the voice as belonging to the taller of the bouncers from the saloon.

"Why shouldn't I be?" Antoinette continued buttoning her blouse. She tried smoothing her skirts, but it was a lost cause. Slocum had wrinkled them too completely to be presentable, but in the darkness the outlaw might not notice.

"Open up. I want to look around."

Antoinette cast a quick glance in Slocum's direction, then opened the door. She stepped back involuntarily when the outlaw bumped into her, knocking her sprawling.

"How dare you!" she raged.

"You see anybody nosin' around?"

"Just you. How rude!"

The outlaw said he wanted to check the place for intruders, but he was taking too much enjoyment watching Antoinette on the floor. Her knees were pulled up, and he might have gotten a glimpse of the paradise usually hidden beneath her skirts. She let out a snort of disgust and pushed down her skirts, then tried to get to her feet, only to slip and sit down heavily again.

"You're looking mighty mussed."

"I was getting ready for bed," she said, "when you interrupted me."

"Need some help gettin' into bed? I'll be glad to tuck

you in." The outlaw leered. "I'll bet we both'd like it if I tucked it in for you."

"Is there anything important you wanted?"

The outlaw saw he wasn't getting anywhere with her. He held out his hand to help her up, but Antoinette ignored him and struggled to stand on her own.

"I have a very busy day planned, unlike some people in Refugio," she said haughtily. "There are children to teach and since your former doctor was hanged, I have to keep hours beyond those usually kept by a physician."

"You want to examine me? I got an ache."

The outlaw let out a gasp as Antoinette stepped back, judged the distance and then kicked him in the balls. He doubled over and gasped for air.

Slocum began fumbling in his boot to find the derringer he had sewn into the inside. He ripped open a seam and touched the cold metal of the small pistol but knew he could never get it out in time if the outlaw turned on Antoinette. He didn't deny that she had been provoked, but the situation was such that it might spell her death.

"Go on, do what you want. Hang me, like you did Dr. Zacharias. It'd be better than putting up with pigs like you. I was brought here to help people, to heal them, to teach children so they won't grow up ignorant savages. That's what Arnot wants from me. I'm not a common Cyprian, *une fille de joie*, a . . . a whore!" Antoinette reared back to kick the man again, but this time he was already on his way to the door.

"Hold your horses," he gasped out. "I didn't mean nothing. It's just that you were so lonesome and all."

"I am not lonesome when I am alone," she said. "I prefer being alone, thank you, to company such as yours."

"You see anyone poking around, you let us know."

"Who, other than you, might that be?"

Slocum tensed.

"We think it's a newcomer to town that's causin' trouble."

"Trouble," sniffed Antoinette. "The only trouble's conjured by the ones who're already here. Now get out and let me get my sleep."

The outlaw left, moving slowly and painfully. Slocum waited until Antoinette slammed the door shut and turned, her back against it.

"That was a close call," he said.

"They're looking for you, John. And they won't stop until they find you."

Slocum's mind raced. "There might be a way to get out of their net. But I'll have to sleep on it."

"Want company?" Antoinette asked impishly.

He did.

15

Slocum didn't know how long he would have to lay low. Perhaps a day or two—or longer. That meant he was going to have to stay alert or one of Arnot's men would plug him. Just before dawn he kissed Antoinette good-bye, then slipped from the doctor's office and returned to the fake depot in the middle of town. The bogus ticket agent, Gustav, slept noisily, head resting on his folded arms. Slocum considered entering the man's small ticket booth and lifting the six-shooter from its place beside him, but he quickly discarded that notion when he found how securely locked the door was. Gustav didn't trust anyone.

In Refugio, Slocum didn't blame him.

Creeping around to the rear where his gear was still stacked on the platform, Slocum studied the area in the first light of dawn to be certain no one watched. The two from the saloon had left Gustav to watch over the belongings waiting here. This allowed Slocum the chance to rummage through the stacks, hunting for anything useful. He found a knife and slipped it into the top of his boot, then settled his pant leg down to hide it. The derringer he had pried loose from inside his boot was tucked away safely into a vest pocket where he could get at it in a hurry, but Slocum knew any shoot-out would end with him being

144

ventilated. A two-shot pistol against a six-shooter was a bad match.

Slocum slipped under the platform and rested, his back against a support. He nodded off waiting for someone to come to the platform to recover their belongings. By nine o'clock he heard a steady tread coming toward him. He peered out and saw the preacher man who had been kidnapped earlier.

"Psst, Parson," Slocum called. When the man of the cloth saw him he looked around in panic. "I need to talk to you."

"My son, you're the one they seek, aren't you?" The preacher squatted down and looked at Slocum's hiding place. "It must be very uncomfortable under there."

"It'll be even more uncomfortable if they put a noose around my neck. You've seen the gallows down the street. That's where I'm bound if they find me."

"What have you done?"

Slocum had worked out his story with Antoinette. He had no trouble lying to a preacher.

"They got me confused with somebody else. The third person they brought here." Slocum pointed to the remaining pile of goods at the end of the platform. He had pawed through the stack and figured whoever had been kidnapped was a banker or bookkeeper. Getting someone else into trouble didn't set well with Slocum, but this was a matter of life and death—and it was more than his life on the line. If he and Antoinette escaped, they could bring the cavalry down on this nest of sidewinders. As pleasant as Refugio looked, it was only a veneer of society. Roiling underneath was cruelty, kidnapping and outright slavery.

"I heard them mention someone else. But if they are wrong, tell them."

"You've seen them, preacher. They're killers."

"But reason with them. They will understand."

"Understand how they've made a mistake? You can tell them they're wrong and they might not do anything. I do it and they plug me. It's not something any man likes to hear, outlaws least of all."

"They are criminals," the preacher said thoughtfully. "This is my God-sent mission. I preached only to those who were converts to the way of God. Here I can find blasphemers, killers, those who have strayed far from the path of righteousness. They are the ones I need to reach with my words and deeds."

"You'd have to have one silver tongue to convince them," Slocum said. "I need to get out of Refugio, away from here." Slocum watched the parson's reaction, gauging how likely the man was to help him. It didn't look promising.

"I have found my calling here," the preacher said. He peered more closely at Slocum. "Do I know you?"

"I'm a patent medicine salesman. Might be you saw me in Parson's Grove or Scott's Bluff. I sell my wares all over western Nebraska."

"I don't remember that," the preacher said, frowning in concentration.

"Then you might have bought some of my elixir back in Omaha." Slocum wanted the preacher to forget the man who had started to board the stagecoach with him, only to go off chasing outlaws. The stage had pulled out, and the preacher had been kidnapped. It wouldn't do to have him ask about Slocum's disguise. He might be a man of God, but Slocum didn't trust him.

"I doubt that."

"Can you ask around, find others who might want to get away? You can stay and preach your Gospel, but some of us aren't too welcome around here."

"That goes against our . . . hosts' wishes."

"Reckon so, but why don't you feel out some of them? Take their measure. You're making the rounds, anyway."

"Why, yes, I am spreading the word. Mr. Arnot has promised me a church, with a steeple and new pews and even hymnals. It seems some of the citizens of this town want to get married properly. How can I deny them such a holy sacrament?"

"Some of the women want to get married," Slocum said under his breath. It amazed him how ordinary Refugio appeared on the surface when it was nothing more than a hideout for some of the worst desperadoes he had ever come across.

"Don't you want to help others?" the preacher asked.

"I want to help those who want to leave. You missed the fact some of the citizens in this town are being held prisoner. You were kidnapped. So were they. So was I."

"But in your instance, don't you want to help others by giving of your medicines? Think of the good you can do."

"I want to spread it around the West," Slocum said. He reached for his vest pocket and the derringer there when he heard the click of boot heels above on the platform.

"What's goin' on down there?" demanded Gustav.

"Ah, my son, I was looking down here for . . . anything I might have dropped," the preacher said, edging back from under the platform. Slocum tensed, waiting to see if the preacher would turn him over to the station agent.

"I ain't your son. I'm old enough to be your pa."

"A manner of speaking. All God's children are of my flock," the preacher said.

Slocum heard Gustav come closer to the edge of the platform. He would have to kneel and look under to see Slocum, but if he did he would get a bullet square between the eyes. Slocum was concerned he might have to use the second round in the derringer on the preacher to keep him from running off with a warning for others in Arnot's gang.

"For a buck I can help you move your gear, padre," Gustav said. "This here pile's yours?"

"It is. But I do not have any money."

"You gotta earn it, like everyone else in Refugio. No money, no help."

"In the service of my Lord, I can transport what is needed."

"Get to it. Anything left here when the next batch of pilgrims comes to town gets sold."

The preacher looked down at Slocum again, nodded once, then jumped to the platform and began putting his belongings into manageable bundles to carry to where his church was to be built. Slocum waited for several minutes after both Gustav and the preacher were gone before poking his head out from under the platform and looking around.

With a boldness that belied the cold knot in his belly, Slocum strode out into Refugio and walked about getting the lay of the land. A quick count showed more men wearing six-shooters than the day before. Once he had to duck into a store when he spotted Big Ed Lawrence and the Dakota Kid coming down the street directly toward him. Slocum noted with some satisfaction that the Kid still moved stiffly, the bullet he had taken slowing him down. Slocum's only regret was not killing him outright.

"Do something for you, mister?"

"I sell medicines. Would you care to put a small display up, near your cash box, perhaps, and split what is sold?"

"Patent medicines?" The storekeeper looked at Slocum, tilted his head to one side and then nervously licked his lips. "Well, I don't know."

"They're looking for me, aren't they?" Slocum asked flatly.

"Yep, they are."

"I haven't done anything wrong. They confused me with another newcomer, but I can't make them believe it. How do I talk to Will Arnot himself?"

"Arnot? You don't want anything to do with him. He likes seeing men die. He likes seeing women die, for all that, and I'm not so sure about children and dogs." The clerk blanched as the words slipped from his lips. Slocum knew that there were people in Refugio who wanted to escape. The clerk was one, although voicing that sentiment was enough to get him strung up.

"Don't worry. I'm looking to get away from here myself," Slocum said.

"I . . . I wouldn't do anything like that. This is a good town. Good."

"Would you help people get out of this valley, even if you like Refugio so much you'd stay?"

Slocum saw the barest nod and knew he had found one reluctant ally. The clerk might never show real backbone when it came to fighting, but if he didn't get into trouble, he would help. A little.

"We'll need supplies for a few days. Not much, nothing that would be missed, but some."

"A burlap bag worth?"

"That'd be appreciated. I'll let you know when."

"I . . . I can leave it out back. So you don't have to come into the store and maybe be seen." The clerk was sweating hard now, but Slocum detected a new resolve. The man had chafed under the yoke put on him by Arnot and his gang long enough and had found a way of fighting back, however feebly.

Slocum glanced out of the store and saw both Lawrence and the Kid had turned into the saloon to drink away the day. A dozen other gun-toting outlaws swaggered up and down the street, but none of them knew Slocum by sight. He took off his glasses and put them into his pocket, then shucked off his coat to disguise himself a little further. He wished he could cut off the short beard and mustache but saw no way of doing it without drawing more attention to himself than was prudent. The barbershop across the street next to the saloon was doing a thriving business, most of the customers wearing six-guns.

His boldness quickly turned foolhardy when Slocum found himself sandwiched between the tall, rawboned bouncer and his nervous partner. Slocum saw no hope for getting away since both men were headed directly for him, but not with determination. He lowered his gaze to the boardwalk, then knelt and began fumbling around. The nervous gunman bumped into him, almost knocking him over.

"Watch where you're takin' a dump," the outlaw growled, giving Slocum another shove. But he went to his partner and the two of them got into an argument. Slocum considered how his luck might hold if he stood and walked off, then decided it wasn't in the cards. They would notice him and one or both would recognize him.

He continued looking down, as if searched for something he had dropped, but his luck ran out.

"It's him!" shouted the nervous gunfighter. The man was fast, but Slocum was already in motion. He dug his toes into the loose planks and shoved hard, sending himself diving parallel to the ground to land in the dusty street. A bullet sang through the air an inch above him.

Slocum rolled back toward the boardwalk and the dubious protection of its overhang. A second bullet slammed through the wood and grazed Slocum's cheek.

By now he had rolled back and got to his feet. He hadn't taken two steps when a heavy body crashed into him, arms circling his knees and bringing him crashing back to the street.

Slocum kicked out, fumbled for his derringer but found his wrist caught in a steely grip.

Slocum used his left fist to pummel the gunman. A glancing blow caught the outlaw on the nose and caused him to recoil, giving Slocum the chance to scramble to his feet. But he found himself ringed in by armed men—all outlaws.

"Don't," the gunman said, wiping blood from his broken nose. "He's mine."

Slocum didn't know if the rangy road agent meant he was going to shoot or fight. Not giving him a chance to draw, Slocum moved in fast and punched hard. His short, quick blows landed on a belly that might have been carved oak. Slocum never gave up, punching harder, faster and then felt himself lifted off his feet by an uppercut. He staggered and fell, sitting in the dust.

"Kill 'im," cried someone in the crowd. "Shoot the varmint."

Slocum kicked, caught his opponent in the knee and brought him to a kneeling position. Slocum kicked again, this time catching the man in the face. By the time they both got to their feet, they were bloody and panting and even more determined to see the fight through. Slocum fought for his life. The gunman fought for his honor.

Slocum took a few punches to the face, then saw his opening. He stepped up and swung a haymaker that knocked out the gunman. Standing over the fallen man, fists still raised, Slocum looked down at his opponent. Then the sky fell on him. The crowd moved in, swinging six-guns and fists and clubs—all aimed at Slocum.

He went down, then he went out.

16

Slocum tried to remember when he had felt such pain and couldn't. There wasn't a square inch of his body that didn't hurt, but it was his head that felt as if it would split wide open like a rotten gourd. Simply breathing sent lances of agony throughout his body, but he concentrated on this to focus his attention. Through force of will, he opened his eyes and blinked. His left eye was almost swollen shut, but he got a good view of the room through his right. It was crowded with outlaws, all standing with hands resting on their six-shooters.

But the room was the doctor's office where he had found Antoinette. He suspected that he was laid out on the examination table but wasn't able to turn and look. Tensing his arms, then relaxing, he moved so his fingers were wrapped around the edges of the table. He heaved, intending to get to his feet and fight his way out.

Nothing happened. He tried again and felt only pain driving like a heated railroad spike into his chest.

"Don't move. You've got a cracked rib," Antoinette said. She leaned over and he saw her only inches away. Her lips moved in some secret message to him alone but a sudden wave of pain clouded his vision and he missed her instructions.

It hardly mattered. All he could do was lie on the table in pain. But Slocum noted that the pain was receding and that, while severe, was more bearable.

"It works, I tell you. I don't know how, but it does. You can't do this to a man who saved your boss's, daughter like he did."

Slocum heard Antoinette speaking but wondered whom she meant. He had done nothing to save anyone. He hadn't been able to save himself. After the pummeling he had received, he had been too stunned to realize the crowd would turn on him.

A buzz of argument was followed by only a few intelligible words. The gist of it was that Arnot's daughter had been ill, and Antoinette had saved her from certain death. Slocum hardly believed the patent medicine he had brought with him to Refugio had any part in this salvation, but he wasn't going to argue the matter. He couldn't.

"Help him sit up. Go on, sir, sit up. You'll be dizzy for a few seconds, then everything will be better."

Strong arms circled his shoulders and pushed him upright. A jolt of pain circled his ribs and then subsided. Slocum took the bottle shoved into his hands so he could take a nip. It tasted awful, but the alcohol braced him.

"See? It helps all manner of ailments," Antoinette said.

"You can't whip up a batch yourself?"

"I'm not actually a doctor. I spend half my time teaching your children, the rest trying to patch up wounds. It was sheer luck a bottle of Dr. Jones's Elixir came into my hands."

"How'd that happen again?"

Slocum turned to get a better look at the questioner. The man was young, almost handsome and well dressed, but there was a coldness about him that chilled the soul. Slocum dropped his feet off the table and fought another wave of dizziness.

"I sold a couple bottles to a guard in that big fortress in the middle of town," he said. "I left a couple more with the storekeeper. And I got another in my coat pocket."

"You had another there," Antoinette said loudly. "I took it and gave it to little Annabelle."

Slocum began putting all the pieces together. Annabelle was Arnot's daughter—and the young man doing the questioning was Will Arnot. Slocum moved to put his hand against his chest, ostensibly to check his ribs but to hunt for the derringer he had secreted in a vest pocket. The vest was missing, as was his jacket and shirt. His fingers rubbed against a plaster holding his ribs in place. Antoinette had fixed him up, as she had others in Refugio. The man he had fought stood to one side glaring at Slocum, his nose taped down where it had been broken in the fight.

"You say he's the one who saved Annabelle?" Arnot asked.

"I knew to give the child the medicine, but he's the one who formulated it," Antoinette said. She stared wide-eyed at Slocum, silently imploring him to go along with the story. He didn't have to be urged to. His life, as well as the woman's, rode on his response.

"I don't know what ailed your daughter," Slocum said, trying to sound as professorial as possible, "but it probably was the grippe. Was she running a fever?"

"Nothing broke it," Arnot said. "Your medicine did."

"That's what I made it for."

"Why'd you try to hightail it out of Refugio when we brought you here?" Arnot demanded.

"I was kidnapped. I had no idea anyone here would need my medicine," Slocum said. "Glad I was of some help."

"Make up more," Arnot ordered. "Annabelle might need it." The outlaw leader hesitated, fixed Slocum with polar-cold eyes and added, "The missus thanks you, too. I'd do anything for her and my daughter." With that, the outlaw pushed through the crowd of gathered crooks and vanished into the night.

Slocum saw the man he had fought fingering the butt of his six-shooter, then come to a decision.

"Get him what he needs so he can cook up a new batch

of that medicine. Willie won't like it if anybody tries to stop him." Then he followed his boss. The others trickled out by ones and twos, some grumbling. One of the last to leave was the gunman with the nervous tic. He came over and thrust his ugly face into Slocum's before speaking.

"You got lucky, mister. We shoulda swung you down at the gallows, but Miss Annabelle's the apple of Arnot's eye. If that medicine of yours ever stops workin', I got dibs on cuttin' you down where you stand."

"It won't stop working," Slocum said. The gunfighter started to leave, then came back, shoving his face into Slocum's again. Slocum fought to keep from recoiling due to the man's bad breath. The outlaw spoke in a voice so low only Slocum could hear.

"That shit of yours, could it cure this twitch of mine?"

"Try it and see," Slocum said. Antoinette had discerned what was going on and handed Slocum a bottle of the witch's brew. Slocum gave it to the gunman, who grunted, shoved it into his pocket and left without another word.

"Was that some of the original batch or something you fixed?" Slocum asked when they were alone.

"Original. I tried one drop of it. It was awful. What did you put into it, other than a lot of alcohol?"

Slocum shrugged. After the beating he had taken it was hard to remember anything as trivial as the recipe for his elixir.

"I didn't actually give it to the little girl. I soaked a rag in it and used it to soothe her fever. It cooled her off, and she rested quietly for the first time in days."

"I can't figure Arnot. He's one mean hombre and here he's talking like he'd kill anyone harming his wife or daughter."

"I heard stories. He's a devoted husband and an even more doting father. I'm not sure but his wife might be the reason Refugio exists. He wouldn't give up thieving, even for her, and she demanded a civilized life."

"Refugio gives them both what they want," Slocum

said. He eased off the table, experienced a flash of vertigo, then got his feet under him.

"They worked you over good, but you gave as good as you took," Antoinette said. He thought there was a hint of pride in her voice.

"I feel like I lost every round."

"You almost did. It's a good thing I passed the word to Arnot that your medicine cured his daughter and that he heard when he did. They don't take kindly to anyone trying to get out of Refugio."

"How many have you talked to with a yen to get out of here?"

Antoinette put her arm around him and guided him to a cot at the side of the room. She sat beside him and pressed her lips close to his ear.

"They might be listening. I think they've been watching me, especially when Arnot brought his daughter here."

"Is she still here?" Slocum looked around the office but saw no trace of a small child. Antoinette might have the girl in her own bedroom.

"Gone home," she said softly. "I've spoken with several people who came to me with ailments. A few of them were obviously frightened, and I didn't pursue the possibility of escape with them, but others were more than fed up being held prisoner by a gang of desperados."

"Most of the townspeople are nothing more than slaves," Slocum said.

"Frightened slaves. Arnot might say he brings their families with them to build a community. Perhaps he even believes it, but it gives a powerful lever against them. Who's man enough to stand against the outlaws when his entire family would pay the price for failure?"

"Even the dog," Slocum said, remembering how he had seen evidence that the outlaws took the baker's dog, along with his family. He had never known the man's name, and now he suspected he was dead.

Antoinette looked at him curiously, then shook her head.

"I talked to three who are willing and who know several others."

"How many can we rely on?"

"Without weapons, who can say? But there will be a dozen men."

Slocum closed his eyes and tried not to dwell on the low number. A dozen against three times that many armed outlaws. And the Arnot gang controlled the powerful citadel in the center of Refugio. From there a mountain howitzer could command the pass out of the valley or destroy any mob large enough to threaten Arnot's control.

Whatever plan they decided on had to involve more stealth than force. Otherwise, the Refugio cemetery would be overflowing with innocents.

"How about the blacksmith? Benbow?"

"You talked to him. He told me. He recognized me and knows I wouldn't steer him wrong. It's awful what they did to him, isn't it?"

"He's a bitter man," Slocum said. "Is he bitter enough to fight them, to help us?"

"Yes."

Slocum's mind raced. A plan formed, but it was a desperate one requiring almost impossible good luck on their part. Try as he might, however, he couldn't think of anything better that was more likely to succeed.

"The stagecoaches they steal and bring in. Does Benbow work on them?"

"Why, yes, I think he does. Most of them are pretty banged up from the trip through the canyon. I've heard others say the canyon walls are very close to the trail."

"I was blindfolded when they brought me in, but I got the sensation I could reach out and touch both walls at the same time when we passed the narrowest sections. Getting a stagecoach out through such a tight gorge is going to be a damn sight harder than getting it in since we're going to have guards shooting at us the whole way."

"Arnot has some plan for the stagecoaches. I'm not sure what, but it has something to do with switching them at depots before big shipments."

"The station agents will load money and mail on the outlaw stage," Slocum said. "Then, when they drive off, nobody will be able to figure out what happened. What station master would ever think that a stagecoach driving up wouldn't belong to the line? A Concord can cost five thousand dollars."

"What are you intending to do with a stagecoach?" Antoinette asked. "I'm sure Benbow would help us, as much as he could. You know he can't get around because of those legs."

"That leg," Slocum amended. He remembered the sight of the wooden peg where a once-healthy limb had been. And the remaining leg was broken so badly Benbow must be in constant pain to remind him of his futile escape attempts.

"He can get us the stage but what of the horses?"

"He makes horseshoes. We might have to wait for him to reshoe a team so we can get both the stage and the horses at his smithy." Slocum didn't like that idea since it meant they had to dance to Arnot's tune. He worried also about Benbow and his reaction. If the crippled blacksmith thought he could fight back, he might spill the beans rather than bide his time.

More than this, Slocum felt the pressure of time weighing him down. Poking a grizzly with a short stick was safer than remaining in Refugio under Willie Arnot's nose.

"Will it work? How can we get into a stagecoach and ride out?" asked Antoinette. "They'd spot us right away."

"There's got to be a way to get a dozen people out at the same time," Slocum said. "That's why I thought the stage might be good."

"It'd make a big target."

Slocum thought hard and decided to scout around Refugio a bit more.

"I'll be back," he said, "but I want to get my shirt and especially the vest."

"Because this was in it?" Antoinette held up the derringer. "You were clever smuggling it in. They are quite thorough searching everyone." The touch of fire in her words told Slocum exactly how furious she was over how the outlaws had treated her.

He dressed carefully, testing the limits of his reach, stretching cramped muscles and finding how far he could bend before his ribs gave him the twinges. All things considered, he was in better shape than his opponent—and the outlaw he had faced in the bare-knuckled fight hadn't been set upon by the crowd.

"Come back when you can, John," she said. "I don't like having to patch you up." Antoinette smiled almost shyly and added, "There are some things I might not be able to stick back together if they get broken." She reached over, her fingers slipping inside his shirt and moving down, stopping only when they reached his tightly cinched belt. The hand slipped away like a breeze in the night.

"I don't know what they expect from me, but I'll be back if I can. Might be they want to see where I spend the night."

"You can always say you're out hunting for ingredients for your medicine and need to return here to mix it up because I have the equipment." Antoinette pointed to the cabinets filled with pestles, mortars and shiny silvered implements of unknown purpose.

"Good idea," Slocum said. He went to the door and signaled her to remain where she was. Carefully opening the door, he peered out. If Arnot had anyone spying on them, he was more cleverly hidden than Slocum could spot.

Slocum hurriedly left, wanting to talk once more with the storekeeper, if he could. The man had promised some help. He might supply more if Slocum convinced him an escape plan could work without endangering the man's family.

As he went down the street toward the general store, Slocum noticed the marshal's office. He remembered the portly outlaw with the shotgun. As much as he didn't want to cross him again, Slocum turned toward the small office in a brick building. In the doorway he stared at the layout. This was the first jailhouse he had ever seen without any cells. He had to remind himself Refugio didn't have a marshal to enforce the law but to keep people from escaping. The entire town was a giant cell. One with pleasant meadows and towering mountains cloaked in purpled distance, but a prison nevertheless.

"What kin I do fer ya?" asked the man behind the desk in the corner of the room.

"Thought I'd look over your wanted posters," Slocum said. If the outlaws considered people enemies, he had to look upon them as possible co-conspirators.

"We give a decent reward fer any of these fellas," the man said. He wore a deputy's badge hammered out of a Mexican silver peso. Slocum saw that there was a nick out of the corner about the size a .45-caliber bullet would make. He wondered if the deputy got this badge by shooting its original wearer through the heart. It wouldn't surprise him.

"How much?" Slocum took the sheaf of paper shoved at him and thumbed through the stack quickly. His eyebrows rose. This wasn't what he had expected.

"We need them folks to fill out our work roster here in Refugio. You know of anybody on the outside, you speak up. There's good money in it if we bring 'em to town on your say-so."

Slocum saw the listing included carpenters, a brick mason, a gunsmith—and a baker.

"You need somebody to bake bread?" Slocum asked.

"Last one, well, let's say he didn't work out so good. Disappointment, too, since he got out one batch that was mighty tasty." The deputy drew his six-gun and laid it on the table to emphasize what had happened to the baker.

"What happened to his family?" Slocum blurted the question before he thought.

"What family?" the outlaw asked coldly.

Slocum turned back to the wanted posters to cover his anger. The baker had been killed—and so had his family. They were no longer necessary to keep the man in line since he had been murdered. Again the peaceful veneer of Refugio cracked and showed the utter callousness beneath.

"Is there a chemist or apothecary in town?" Slocum asked. "I need some special ingredients and can't find them at the general store."

"Nope, ain't got any of them fellows. You might take up in that perfession, though, and make yerself even more indispensable, if you catch my meaning."

Slocum did. He was on probation and wasn't likely to be found necessary in the end, even if Antoinette had lied about his medicine saving Arnot's daughter.

"I can do a job like that. Making my elixir's not so different from running an apothecary shop. I'd need stock for the store. How would I go about getting it when all I've got are a couple dollars?"

"You'd have to tell your tale to the boss. If he decides Refugio needs what you can offer, he'll set you up with stock and a store along the main street."

"Right nice of him," Slocum said dryly.

"That's the way it is in Refugio. You pull your weight, you get along jist fine."

Slocum continued flipping through the "Wanted Posters" and an idea came to him full-blown and ready to put into effect. And all he needed were items both the storekeeper and the blacksmith could provide.

"Thanks," Slocum said. "You've been a help."

"Be seeing you," the deputy said, hand resting on the pistol he had placed on the desk.

Slocum's lips curled into a smile as he left. He doubted the deputy or anyone else in Refugio would be seeing much more of him if his plan worked.

17

"How much kerosene do you need, John?" Antoinette Thibadeaux looked anxious. "The storekeeper's balking at giving any more. Arnot keeps a close watch on everything sold in Refugio."

"His new bookkeeper does, at any rate," Slocum said. The third man who had arrived about the time Slocum and the preacher did had worked overtime to prove himself worthy of his position. Slocum had seen him in the store, taking inventory, grilling the storekeeper about his sales. If they couldn't get the storekeeper to give them more kerosene, Slocum wondered if they could bribe the bookkeeper.

Antoinette read his mind. "He's utterly incorruptible," she said. "I approached him and used a bit of my feminine wile. He wouldn't have anything to do with me."

"He's not incorruptible," Slocum said. "He's dead. Maybe above and below the waist."

"You're so sweet, John." She brushed his arm with hers and clever fingers contrived to slip inside his jacket and stroke over his belly with a hint of movement lower. Antoinette quickly moved away so no one would see. It wouldn't pay for any of Arnot's men to start gossiping about Antoinette and the patent medicine peddler.

"Not sweet, just committed to the truth," he said. Antoinette grinned even more at this as they strolled along the boardwalk on the street opposite to the saloon.

Slocum had hunted for a second saloon and had not found one. That meant Arnot concentrated his men into one watering hole, whether to keep track of them or to keep down drunkenness was a matter of conjecture. There didn't seem to be any detail of life in Refugio that Will Arnot did not control directly. Rather than finding that restricting, Slocum intended to use it to his own advantage and bring the cavalry down on the outlaw hideout.

"What do they keep in that?" Antoinette stared at the fortress in the center of town.

"I reckon they keep their loot there," Slocum said. His mind returned to the reason he had gotten involved in all this. Pierre Thibadeaux and his Bible had set the clockwork into motion. Now it was time for Slocum to throw a wrench into the works. But if he could do it after he retrieved Antoinette's legacy Bible, he would.

"They've been ravaging the countryside for almost a year," she said. "They must have accumulated an impressive stash."

He heard the greed in her voice and didn't blame her. The way Arnot maintained the arsenal in that fortress meant there was likely a small mountain of gold hidden inside. Some of it would go a long way toward paying him for the time and trouble he'd gone to already.

"There's no telling if your Bible is there," Slocum said. "Fact is, it's probably not. When the outlaws saw what they had, they probably threw it away on the way back here."

"I have to know." Antoinette let out a deep sigh. "I'd almost forgotten this was the reason for taking on the Arnot gang."

"Not the only reason," Slocum said. He remembered all too well how the lawmen in the surrounding towns had either hightailed it or looked the other way. He wasn't even certain the U.S. Army would be interested in stopping Arnot, what with their interest in the Sioux uprising paramount.

"How do you intend to sneak a look in there?" Antoinette asked.

"I've got an idea, but it depends on timing. And you'll have to help."

Antoinette looked over her shoulder and said, "We'd better move along. We're attracting attention."

Slocum saw the bouncer from the saloon had come out, the white bandage across the bridge of his nose gleaming in the bright Nebraska sun. The gunman he had fought was nowhere to be seen. Slocum hoped the elixir had given him a bellyache.

What he wished for more than dealing out a bellyache or a broken nose was his Colt Navy firmly in his grip, facing these men.

"We have to be careful since they are watching us," Antoinette said, smiling prettily and waving to the gunman. He didn't acknowledge her presence but Slocum noted that the man's cold eyes never left them as they walked back down the street toward the doctor's office, away from the citadel in the middle of town.

"They watch everyone," Slocum said. But he knew she was right. They were being carried along in a bubble of Arnot's favor right now because his daughter had gotten better. The instant that protective bubble burst, lead would fly and Slocum and Antoinette would be dead. He touched the tight bandage wrapped around him and knew that soon his body might be encircled by something even tighter—a hangman's noose. Blood sport passed for entertainment in Refugio.

"I can mix up something for you. We have enough ingredients, if you'll talk to a few more men. I'm not sure they'd take kindly to a woman offering to get them out of here."

"You mean the barber and the barkeep and others who are surrounded by the gang?"

"Them. Some of the others who tend the horses might be good to cultivate friendships with also," Antoinette said. The lovely dark-haired woman sounded a little shrill, as if the strain was getting to her. Slocum didn't bother telling her he had already decided not to approach anyone working in the livery stables because they were the most likely to be firmly in Arnot's hip pocket. They might not wear shooting irons on their hips, but they were a part of his gang, a part of Refugio's power structure devoted to keeping everyone securely imprisoned. Nobody escaped this valley without a horse, and the men tending the horses had to be the most loyal.

"Go on, get back to the office," Slocum said. "I'll see what I can do." His mind already raced ahead, figuring how to get rid of the broken-nosed outlaw who had crossed the street and now followed closely. Slocum hesitated when Antoinette went straight ahead, then cut down a side street. He paused in front of the small bookstore and caught the reflection of the outlaw trailing him. He had hoped the man would have either followed Antoinette or given up and returned to the saloon.

Slocum went into the store and looked around, a half-formed notion that whoever had stolen the Bible might have put it into the store to sell. There weren't any Bibles, and nothing else in the small store caught his eye. He turned and looked at the window display from inside and saw the outlaw with the broken nose lounging about outside, waiting for him.

"You have any more books?" Slocum asked the proprietor, not bothering to turn to look at the man.

"Got a new shipment in the back room I haven't unpacked yet, but most all of them's duplicates of what's on the shelves here."

"I'll take a look, if you don't mind."

"Something special you need?"

Slocum pushed through the door into the storage room. Boxes stacked head-high blocked the back door. He pushed them aside, as if looking for something in particular.

"Anything on herbs and medicinal roots," he said.

"Nope, don't have anything like that. Mostly, we get

books for the ladies in town. And the school kids. Mr. Arnot is insistent that they all have the best books for their education."

"Thoughtful man, Arnot," Slocum said, getting the last box moved aside.

"His wife's the one who insists, but whatever she wants, he asks for."

Slocum doubted anything Arnot "asked" for was couched in polite terms. More likely, it had the full force of his outlaw gang behind it.

"I'll check back when you get a new shipment," Slocum said, opening the rear door and hastily leaving. He heard the proprietor protest the use of the door, then he was cut off by distance. Slocum loped along, heading for the black-smith's shop. He didn't fully trust Benbow to go along with any plan without trying to exact his own revenge, but Slocum didn't have a huge number of townspeople to choose from when asking for aid.

He stopped and cast a quick glance over his shoulder before ducking into the smithy. Benbow worked diligently at his forge, his face set in a look that combined anger with resignation. The blacksmith looked up when he heard Slocum step closer.

"You ready?" was all he asked.

"Not yet. I need to look over the stage. It's out back?"

"Been workin' on the wheel. They busted it up something fierce. Not a good cartwright in town, so I'm doin' what I can," Benbow said. He hobbled around the forge, lifting a long strip of red-hot iron from the fire. Slocum recognized that eventually it would be hammered and bent into a rim for a wagon wheel. For the moment, Benbow took his time, giving Slocum the chance to put his plan for escape into action.

But how long the smith could stall forced Slocum's hand. It wouldn't do having the men helping him with his mad scheme also ending up at the end of Arnot's noose.

"Are the bags from the general store out back?" asked Slocum.

"Stored behind a pile of pig iron ingots," Benbow said. "Six bags. What's in 'em?"

"Our escape," Slocum said. He checked the street outside the shop and didn't see the gunman who had been trailing him, then ducked out back. Rummaging through the heavy bars of iron took all his strength. More than once his ribs gave a sharp jolt of pain, but Slocum kept working. This might be the last time he had a chance before everything had to be set into motion.

Once the ingots were moved aside, he saw the six burlap bags that had been hidden from prying eyes. He grabbed two and lugged them to the stagecoach, opened the door and began positioning them inside. Leather straps on the compartment floor normally secured either a strongbox or other cargo. Slocum used these to hold down his sacks. Quickly returning to the hiding place, he dragged two more to the stagecoach. His stamina was waning fast, telling him how bad the beating actually had been. He had been running on nothing but determination and now his body was rebelling. Slocum filed this away as something to consider when the actual escape was made.

He made one last trip to the hiding place and divvied up the contents of the burlap bag between the boot of the stagecoach and the driver's box. Carefully covering his handiwork with the emptied bags, he jumped to the ground. His legs gave way under him—and this saved his life.

If he had remained on his feet, the bullet would have blown the top off his head. As it was, he felt the passage of deadly lead but the splinters flying from the side of the stage produced the worst injury.

Slocum swung about, his hand going to the derringer hidden in his vest pocket. Unused to the small weapon, he fumbled a mite. A second slug tore through the air in his direction. Slocum wasn't sure where it ended up, but as long as it wasn't in his gut or head, he was happy to let the outlaw blow the stagecoach into smithereens.

Falling flat, Slocum rolled under the coach and finally got

the derringer into his grip. He cocked the hammer and tried to sight in on a good target, but the outlaw was moving fast.

"Why're you shooting?" Slocum called, wanting the man to hesitate. "I was just helping out the blacksmith."

"You lyin' son of a bitch," came the angry words. "I knew you were up to no good. You're going to use that stage to escape from Refugio."

"Why'd I do a thing like that?"

Slocum wiggled around and used one of the wheels for a barricade against new bullets. It was hardly adequate, which he found out fast as two more slugs ripped past spokes and kicked up dust on either side of his body. Slocum held his fire. The derringer's range wasn't enough to make an accurate shot possible until he got within a few feet of his target.

By then he might be dead.

Slocum feinted right and then rolled left, heading for the front of the stagecoach. He winced as another shot grazed his arm. He reached the front, got behind the stage and pulled himself up painfully into the driver's box. This gave him height but still no decent shot at the outlaw intent on ventilating him.

Crouching in the box, Slocum waited. He couldn't see out, and the sides of the box fit together too well to give him a peephole. Waiting for the outlaw to reload and then rush him was hard to do, but Slocum had no choice. He felt weak all over and could never outrun the outlaw, much less the bullets flying from his six-shooter.

He quieted his pounding heart, took off the violet-colored glasses and tucked them in his pocket, then counted slowly. Slocum imagined how long it would take for the man behind the blacksmith's shop to grow impatient, then venture out. Since Slocum hadn't shot back, a wrong assumption might be made. No shot, no gun. Slocum depended on that mistake.

When he reached twenty, Slocum popped up, aimed the derringer and saw the startled expression on the outlaw's face. His eyes went wide on either side of his broken nose with its snow-white bandage. Then those eyes rolled up, the outlaw threw out his arms and flailed about before hitting the ground hard.

Slocum's first shot had caught the road agent squarely in the middle of his forehead. Tucking his derringer back into his vest, Slocum started to jump to the ground. The outlaw's fallen pistol would make a good addition to his arsenal, such as it was. But from the other side of the smithy came loud cries and the sound of running men.

Slocum judged how fast he could reach the dead outlaw and retrieve his six-gun, then knew he would be caught bending over the body. Spinning, he went over the back side of the driver's box, hit the ground and lit out running as fast as his wobbly legs would take him. When he reached a pile of coal intended to fuel the forge in Benbow's shop, he dived forward and landed hard. A cinder lodged in the back of his hand, stinging mightily.

But Slocum did not stir. He listened to the uproar when the other outlaws found their dead partner.

He hoped they didn't poke around the stagecoach and see what he had done to it—and he hoped they wouldn't come looking for him right away. He had the one shot left. That was hardly enough to take out a posse of angry outlaws. He might as well turn the derringer on himself and save prolonged agony from whatever torture they'd mete out—and the eventual hanging. "Where'd the killer go?"

"Must be one of us," spoke up a voice Slocum recognized all too well. It sent a chill up his spine as Big Ed Lawrence took charge of the search.

Luckily for Slocum, Lawrence made the mistake of believing one of his cohorts had done the killing and immediately set about checking every outlaw's six-shooter. This gave Slocum the opportunity to sneak away unnoticed.

By the time he reached Antoinette's office, there was chaos everywhere in the town of Refugio. All the outlaws were intent on finding the killer of one of their gang.

18

"The whole town's in an uproar," Antoinette said, peering out the window in the doctor's office. Slocum settled down on the examination table, stretched and tried to get the pain to ease. He had banged himself up in the fight with the saloon bouncer. Most of all he wished he had snared the fallen man's six-shooter. It wasn't going to do the dead outlaw any good anymore and it could mean the difference between life and death for Slocum.

"Not the whole town," Slocum said, stretching and testing the limits of his body. It felt barely tolerable but would be better with a swig of the patent medicine he had brewed up. That had enough whiskey in it to stun an ox. "Just the outlaws."

"There's no difference," Antoinette insisted. "They will begin killing those who are captives unless they find the man who shot—"

"You mean until they find me," Slocum said grimly. His mind raced. It wouldn't be long until Arnot or his henchmen came around looking for the killer. They had to concoct a story to put any doubts the outlaws had to rest. Slocum wasn't sure how to do that.

"They're coming," Antoinette said breathlessly. "A half dozen of them. The man with the twitch is leading them."

171

"At least it's not Lawrence," Slocum said. He had successfully avoided the outlaws who might identify him as someone other than a patent medicine peddler.

"What are we going to do?" Antoinette sucked in her breath, causing her breasts to rise gloriously under her blouse. This was all the inspiration Slocum needed for a reasonable alibi.

He tore off his shirt and kicked free of his boots. He was dropping his pants as he advanced on Antoinette. She stared at him openmouthed.

She cried out when he grabbed a double handful of blouse and yanked hard, ripping free the garment. Buttons skittered about the floor and came to rest in odd corners of the office. She was naked to the waist, but this wasn't good enough for Slocum. He ran his fingers under the waistband of her skirt and twisted brutally, ripping the cloth.

The skirt fell about her ankles.

"What are you doing, John?"

"Quiet," he said, spinning her around so fast she reached out and caught herself on the desk. He moved behind her quickly, shoving his groin into the white rounded curves of her rump. Slocum reached around and caught one dangling breast just as the door exploded inward, kicked open by the stocky outlaw with the facial twitch.

"What're you doing?" he demanded. He stopped and stared at a naked Antoinette and a mostly exposed Slocum in such a compromising position.

"Can't you tell?" Slocum grated out.

"Get out, get out!" screeched Antoinette. She tried to cover up. "Isn't there *any* privacy in this horrid town?" Antoinette coyly covered her breasts but left other parts of her anatomy exposed to good effect. The men crowded in to get a better look. Slocum reckoned not a one remembered why they had burst into the office.

"You been at this long?"

"Since I was knee-high to a grasshopper," Slocum shot

back, letting anger enter his voice as he intentionally misinterpreted the question. "And the lady doesn't have to answer such an impertinent question."

"Not what I meant. I mean, you two, now, how long? Never mind." He turned and held out his arms, herding the men behind him back into the street. He closed the door, although it hung at a crazy angle, the top hinge broken from his forceful entry.

"Whew," sighed Antoinette. "That was quick thinking. I'm glad it worked. What do we do now?"

Slocum smiled.

"They know what it looked like we were doing. Why don't we keep going?"

"Oh, you men! Is that all you ever—oh!" Antoinette gasped when Slocum's hand lightly caressed her breasts and then danced downward to the fleecy triangle hidden between her legs. She sagged back in reaction, her legs parting slightly.

"This might be the last time for a while," he said. Slocum thought it might be the last time ever if the escape attempt failed. More than that, it seemed the perfect way to take his mind off his aches and pains and the nearness of death.

Antoinette kissed him to let him know her answer. Pressed close, their bodies began to sweat. The slickness lubricated them as they moved and glided and stroked over each other's body, exploring and stimulating and teasing. Slocum eventually guided Antoinette back to the desk. She sat on the edge and hiked her feet up, opening herself wantonly to him, but this wasn't what he wanted.

"I want to finish it the way I started," he said, kissing her lips and throat. Antoinette leaned back, allowing him to move lower as he licked and suckled at her breasts. He used his tongue to lightly bat about the cherry-bright nubs atop each mound of snowy flesh, then worked lower between those tempting mountains. His tongue dipped into the well of her navel and slithered lower to the darkly tangled mat below. This oral attention caused Antoinette to lie flat on the desk.

Then she let out a yelp as Slocum grabbed her legs and expertly flipped her onto her belly as easily as if he was in a bulldogging competition. The difference was in what he did next. He pulled her back so her legs dangled down, her toes touching the floor, her body flat against the surface of the desk.

He moved in quickly behind her. Before he had been flaccid and pretending. Now his manhood throbbed with need. His groin pressed firmly into the soft flesh of her buttocks as he speared forward. He found the moist crevice he sought, paused a moment to get his balance and then gently entered inch by agonizingly delectable inch until he was fully hidden in her.

Slocum relished the warmth and tightness about him. Antoinette moaned and began moving her hips just a little, lifting them off the desk and thrusting backward in a vain attempt to get more of his length within her. This movement sent ripples of carnal desire into Slocum's loins. He withdrew carefully, then reentered her with more speed, more determination. Antoinette gasped in delight.

He bent over and grabbed her hips with both hands to get more leverage. He began rocking to and fro, driving deeper into her steamy core with every stroke. Her hips spiralled about and he sank directly into the erotic bull's-eye from behind. The combination of movement pushed both of their desires to the breaking point quickly.

Antoinette cried out in release and sank down while Slocum was still poling away. The sudden grasp around his buried shaft and the sound of her excitement pushed him over the edge. He spewed forth his seed. The world spun about him and then slowly returned to normal. He stepped back and looked down at the still prone woman dangling over the edge of the desk. It was probably the best use the furniture had ever been put to.

"Oh, John, that was so intense," Antoinette said. Hips still pressed against the edge of the desk, she pushed up with her hands and bent her back like a cat stretching in the sun. "More. I want more."

"I do, too," he said, "but it'll have to wait."

"For what?" Antoinette rolled over and kept her legs invitingly wide.

"For a treat after we get away from Refugio." This acted like cold water thrown in the woman's face.

"You're right, damn you," she said. "What do we do?"

"Get the people together as soon as the furor dies down," Slocum said. "Then we'll make a break for it."

He went to the cabinet where the doctor had kept his supplies and pawed through until he found a small bottle. He took out a bit of his own patent medicine potion and added the doctor's drug. With a firm motion, he recorked the bottle before tucking it into his coat pocket.

"I don't know if I'm up for it, John. Maybe you should have somebody else go along."

"Like the preacher man?" Slocum almost snorted in disgust. He worried what the parson might do. It might be a good idea to have the preacher with them to keep an eye on him, but Slocum knew they had to move fast and do the escape right the first time. They wouldn't get a second chance.

"Why not?"

"You can ride a horse. Get changed."

"Well, I'm already halfway there," Antoinette said, smiling. Naked she made a small pirouette, curtsied and laughed as she hurried to the bedroom. In less than ten minutes she returned dressed in dark men's clothing.

"Good thing we're doing this at night. Nobody'd ever confuse you with a man."

"Why, thank you, I think," she said, pulling her Stetson down and tucking her long dark locks underneath.

"All you need to finish the disguise is a gun belt and six-shooter."

Antoinette looked out the window. "It's getting toward twilight, John." Her nervousness began to show in the way her voice quavered just a bit. "Should we go?"

Slocum touched the derringer resting in his vest pocket, checked to be sure he had the bottle of elixir and then nodded. He hoped everything worked out well. The plan was simple enough but he needed the help of those he and Antoinette had recruited.

They slipped from the office and made their way through gathering shadows to the general store. The shopkeeper was just closing when he saw them.

"Now," Slocum said. "Start a ruckus now."

"Hard to match the one an hour or two back," the proprietor said.

"What's going on?" came a shrill voice.

"Good thing you chanced by, parson," Slocum said. He pushed Antoinette behind him and around the corner of the store to keep her out of sight. "Time's ripe. Let's go now. Like we agreed on."

"I . . . I don't know," the preacher said. "There are so many souls to save here."

"They're holdin' the whole damned lot of us prisoners! We're hardly more than their slaves!" raged the proprietor. "Help save *our* souls!"

"Yes, of course, but they will kill us all if they find out what we're up to."

"They might kill us anyway, just for sport," the storekeeper said, his dander up now. "Go get the others. Tell them all. I'll rustle up a few more for a good-sized crowd."

"Go on, Parson," Slocum said. "There won't be much bloodshed if we do this quick."

"Very well," the preacher said, turning away.

"John," whispered Antoinette. "Don't let him go. He's going to betray us!"

Slocum drew the derringer from his vest and aimed at the preacher's back, but two outlaws burst from the saloon and crossed his line of fire. Slocum faded back into the alley with Antoinette.

"Let's hope he doesn't—" The words were hardly out of Slocum's mouth when he heard the preacher calling out.

"Mr. Lawrence! I have something to tell you. Promise not to harm any of them and I'll tell you what they intend doing. The doctor and the medicine peddler."

"John!" gasped Antoinette. "He's going to ruin everything."

Slocum watched as the preacher spoke with great animation to Big Ed Lawrence. The gunman nodded, then barked orders to those inside the saloon. A dozen or more outlaws came spilling out. Then Lawrence drew his six-shooter and fired a single shot into the preacher's face.

"The others aren't giving in," Slocum shouted to the outlaws. The outraged storekeeper swung a board and smashed an outlaw in the back of the head. Then others in the crowd rushed forward, braving the gunfire from the outlaws. Several were wounded but others wrested six-shooters from the hands of the desperadoes. A full-scale riot was in the making.

Slocum waited for one outlaw to come rushing past; he was trying to circle the crowd in the street and get a better shot at the men in the back. Slocum slugged him, stripped off his gun belt, hefted the pistol and then tossed everything to Antoinette.

"Put it on. We've got some horse-stealing to do."

Slocum ran, not bothering to let Antoinette keep up. He had work to do, and there was scant time to do it. The crowd would be quelled quickly enough and by that time, he had to be driving like a madman for the pass leading from Refugio's valley. The corral where the outlaws kept their horses was usually guarded, but not tonight, not with outlaws being gunned down and the townspeople kicking up a fuss. Slocum saddled one horse and cut out four others for a stagecoach team. He worked steadily but still felt as if Will Arnot's hot breath gusted down his neck.

He swung into the saddle and led the other four horses

from the corral, not bothering to replace the latch on the gate. If the horses scattered, that only added to the confusion. Glancing over his shoulder, he saw that one building—the saloon?—had been set afire. He grinned wolfishly. The more destruction in Refugio's streets, the better the chance for escape.

He galloped up to where the stagecoach loomed dark and ominously silent behind Benbow's shop. The blacksmith was nowhere to be seen but with his gimpy leg—and a peg on the other—his usefulness was over. Getting the stage ready to roll was as much as the smith could do, and more than Slocum had expected.

"John!" cried Antoinette. "I was getting worried."

"I came as fast as I could."

"The fire, in town, it's spreading."

"Don't worry about it."

"But people are hurt. I ought to—"

"You ought to get the hell away from here so you can save even more," Slocum said harshly. "Let them die now. You'll be saving their families."

He worked frantically to hitch the team to the stagecoach, then lashed the saddle horse to the rear of the stage. "Inside. Do exactly as we planned."

"John, this isn't going to work."

"It will, if you don't lose your nerve."

Shots rang out. Whether they were directed at Slocum and Antoinette didn't matter. They were close. Slocum scrambled into the driver's box, snapped the reins, got the team pulling and lurched away from town. He cut across the meadows until he found the single road leading to the narrow canyon and freedom.

"But the guards, John. How many will there be?"

"Who knows? What does it matter? Get your mask up and pull down your hat. Get ready." He whipped the horses mercilessly. Their flanks quickly lathered, but he kept them at a full gallop. He had to reach the mouth of the canyon before pursuit from the town developed.

As he neared the forebodingly dark pinnacles on either side of the road through the canyon, he slowed, giving the horses a breather.

"Break those jars. Do it now, slosh the kerosene over everything inside." His nose wrinkled at the pungent odor of coal oil rising from inside the compartment as Antoinette obeyed. He stomped down hard and broke the bottles he had placed in the driver's box. Some spattered the legs of his pants, but he hoped this wouldn't matter. When they were fifty yards from the mouth of the canyon, he pulled hard on the reins and stopped the coach. He wanted to give the guards plenty of time to know something unusual was happening. He wanted to draw them from their sentry points to see.

Leaping to the ground, he ran around and smashed the bottles of kerosene he had put in the boot. The liquid dribbled down onto the ground, forcing him to step away.

"You ready?"

"Yes, John, as ready as I'll ever be." Antoinette climbed from the stagecoach and started toward him, then turned suddenly and darted for the canyon mouth. He heaved a deep sigh. She had only to blend in with the sentries. The hard part lay ahead.

Taking the reins of the saddle horse, he led it around to the side of the stage, then climbed into the driver's box. With a loud "yeehaw!" he got the exhausted team pulling hard and fast again. A few ragged shots from hesitant guards ripped through the air around him. Slocum kept his head down and the team pulled hard.

Then he drew his derringer, pointed it at the floor of the driver's box and fired.

The roar of flames leaping up engulfed him and almost caused him to pass out from lack of air. Slocum jerked to one side, gave the frightened horses another quick snap of the reins and jumped. He hit the saddle of the horse running alongside so hard it took his breath away.

He was conscious enough to veer away from the canyon

mouth, only dimly aware of all that happened. The stage-coach had turned into an inferno by the time it reached the mouth of the canyon. The frightened horses kept pulling until it clattered against a rocky wall and tipped over. They continued to pull burning shards of the coach after them as they plunged deeper into the canyon, creating total chaos among the guards.

Slocum shook off the muzziness in his head and realized pain was creeping up his own legs. Reaching down, he swatted out the fire burning at his cuffs. He kept riding hard at a right angle to the road and managed to avoid the thundering posse of outlaws from Refugio heading for the canyon to cut off any escape.

He hoped Antoinette Thibadeaux had mingled with the guards unnoticed and was making her way undetected to the far side of the pass. If she had been caught, what he had to do next would be for naught.

Slocum rode back to Refugio and the hell fires burning there.

19

Slocum came upon Refugio from the direction opposite the canyon. He heard sporadic gunfire and saw that the stagecoach still blazed brightly in the canyon mouth. He wished he knew if Antoinette had escaped through the pass, disguised as one of the guards, but there was no way to know that until she returned with a company of cavalry.

If she returned.

Slocum tried to keep an optimistic frame of mind as he hit the ground, stumbled a few steps, then recovered his balance. There wasn't anywhere to hide the horse, so he didn't bother. He tethered it in front of the citadel and wondered how many guards Arnot had posted inside. From the way half of Refugio smoldered, he guessed most of the citizens were busy trying to keep the other half of town from burning to the ground. And the outlaws would be trying to plug the canyon with their bullets and bodies. It wouldn't take them too long to figure out nobody had been in the stage when it had exploded into flames. That would bring Arnot and the rest of his gang back to town. Slocum had to be ready for them when they came.

He pressed his hand into the patch pocket on the side of his jacket, smoothed wrinkles from his clothing and realized that he had lost his violet-tinted "professor" glasses.

He ignored this as he walked boldly to the peephole in the side of the fortress now commanding Refugio as it never had before. Not twenty feet away a building had been gutted, leaving only a brick shell.

"Hello!" Slocum called. "Anybody in there?" He tried to keep from smiling when the peephole opened and a familiar face peered out.

"You, the snake oil salesman," the guard said. "Whatcha want? The whole damned town's in an uproar. You oughta be findin' yerself a burrow to hide in."

"And leave my customers without their medicine?" Slocum pulled the bottle of elixir from his pocket and held it up. "I brought it specially for you, since the earlier doses appeared to do you a world of good."

He saw the guard's reaction. The man wiped his lips with the back of his sleeve.

"Ain't got money to pay for it, not this time."

"You can't dip into the treasure chests in that fine structure, not even for medicinal remedies that will keep you alert?" asked Slocum. He would gladly give the bottle to the guard but had to make it appear he was more interested in money than curatives.

"I kin owe you."

"Two dollars," Slocum said. "If I allow you to partake of this exquisite medicine, you'll have to pay me two dollars."

"Done," the guard agreed readily. "Gimme."

Slocum advanced slowly and held out the bottle, trying to figure the best way to proceed. He gave it over. The guard snatched it from his grip and popped the cork. Slocum heard gurgling sounds as the man chugged the contents. Slocum caught his breath. He hadn't anticipated this.

"Don't drink it too fast. I mixed up an extra special batch. You're likely to get a bellyache something fierce," he said, trying to come up with a malady that would bring the guard to one of the barred doorways. "It can give you the dropsy and grippe, not to mention a fever and make you powerful dizzy."

"Yeah, I . . . I'm kinda dizzy. World's spinnin' 'round 'n round."

"I must give you an antidote immediately or your dick'll fall off!" Slocum was frantic now to get the man to pull back the locking bar.

"Don't . . . can't have that," the guard said.

Slocum heard the grating of wood against wood as the bar slid away. He didn't hesitate when he saw the door open the barest amount. He slammed his shoulder hard into the door and fell into the fortress. Scrambling to his feet, he prepared for a fight. The guard had slumped down, unconscious. Before checking him, Slocum closed the door and replaced the heavy locking bar.

The guard's breathing was ragged and his pupils were dilated. Slocum had put the full bottle of chloral hydrate into his own elixir. The knockout drops had worked quick and would keep the man out of the fight for a day or longer. Just to be sure, Slocum tied him up, then looked around. A single dim kerosene lamp shone its pale yellow light on the crates stacked around the large room. He made a quick inventory, then went up to the second floor. He whistled when he saw the arms stored here. Arnot didn't have one mountain howitzer but four, one on each wall. Slocum worked to load all four, then made sure the shot, gunpowder and wadding were conveniently positioned near each small cannon for quick reloading.

He went to the roof and saw the full firepower available to those who had reached the safety of this presidio. Not only did Arnot have a Gatling gun, he had crates of dynamite for bombs on all four walkways around the third story. Slocum guessed he would need some of this firepower soon and lit two more kerosene lamps so he wouldn't have to fumble with a lucifer in the heat of battle.

Barely had he finished his preliminary scouting of the fortress when he saw Arnot and his gang come galloping back. Whether the outlaw leader realized what had happened or was merely playing it safe, Slocum didn't know.

Will Arnot rode directly for the doors leading into the fortress and bellowed something Slocum didn't understand.

Swinging the Gatling gun about on its tripod and aiming downward, Slocum began turning the crank. He sent a firestorm of .45 caliber slugs ripping through the assembled gang of outlaws, scattering them to the four winds. Try as he might, Arnot wasn't able to get control of his men.

When Slocum had run out of ammo for the Gatling gun, he began lighting bundles of dynamite and tossing them off each side of the fort. Then he hurried down to the second floor, reaching the first of the mountain howitzers about the time the first bundle of dynamite exploded. The concussion rocked even the sturdy walls of the fortress, but the pounding noise of the first howitzer firing dwarfed even the roar of the dynamite.

Slocum hurried around, firing each cannon as quickly as he could, wanting the outlaws to think their citadel had been captured by a dozen or more desperate men. He added a few rounds from a rifle he had picked up and made his way back to the roof. He had been a sniper during the war and knew he could pick off one or two of the less cautious road agents.

As he slowly scanned the streets of Refugio, he saw nothing moving. The outlaws had hightailed it.

For the time being. Slocum knew Arnot wouldn't allow anyone—even an army of men—to occupy the heart of his power. It was late at night and the only light in Refugio came from buildings still on fire. Come dawn, he would have a real fight on his hands.

Slocum went around, loading rifles and leaving them where he could reach them quickly, then reloaded the cannon and went to the bottom floor. He had seen a large iron-bound chest in the center of the room. Working with a crowbar failed to open the strongbox but a half stick of dynamite blew off a hinge, giving Slocum the way into the box.

As he shoved back the lid, his eyes widened. He had

seen piles of gold before, jewels and greenbacks and about everything that was valuable but never had he seen so much stacked in one place. And strangely, on top of the riches stolen by Arnot and his gang over the past year lay a Bible.

Antoinette Thibadeaux's Bible.

Before he could take it from the strongbox he heard gunfire outside. Slocum raced all the way to the third story and grabbed a rifle. Arnot had mustered enough of his gang to launch an attack. Slocum fired steadily, emptying one rifle and discarding it in favor of another, as he went from one wall to the next.

Then came the return fire that forced him to keep his head down. He spent the next few hours firing the cannons, shooting at moving shadows and trying to stay alive.

"Give it up!" came Arnot's shout at dawn's first light. "You leave, we let you live. If we have to dig you out, I swear, you're going to suffer!"

Slocum didn't believe the outlaw for an instant. If he opened the door without a fight, he was dead. Better to go down fighting. He hurried around the perimeter on the second floor, firing the cannons in sequence, then returned to the third story to get as many of them as possible before they got into the fortress.

But he had hardly fired a dozen rounds when he heard another sound, a distant bugle, a trumpeting of a cavalry unit in full charge. Slocum shielded his eyes and looked toward the pass. All he saw was a dust cloud. Then, quickly, he made out the company pennant flying at the head of a column of several dozen soldiers. Hardly knowing he did so, he let out a cheer of triumph. Seldom had he been so eager to see Yankee soldiers riding toward him.

In five minutes the cavalry from Fort Robinson had surrounded the citadel and, twenty minutes later, he stood talking to Captain Dawson. To his great surprise, Sheriff Quince rode with the soldiers—and Antoinette Thibadeaux.

"I found the sheriff camped outside the pass, John," she said, coming to his arms and clinging to him. "He'd found the way in but didn't have the men to launch an attack. I convinced Captain Dawson to come."

"Her brother was a good soldier," Dawson said stiffly. "It was the least I could do for his relative."

"He wouldn't listen to me about Arnot and his boys," the sheriff grumbled. "But a pretty little filly turns his eye."

"It was you I overheard arguing with the sheriff," Slocum said, remembering his stint in the Parson's Grove jail cell. He had thought Quince night be in cahoots with Arnot but he had been trying to convince the army officer to go after the road agents plaguing northwestern Nebraska.

The captain and the sheriff began arguing over jurisdiction and who would get credit for capturing Will Arnot. Slocum didn't bother pointing out that the outlaw leader had eluded them and was probably escaping along a secret path out of the valley, but that was no longer his concern. He tugged on Antoinette's arm and separated her from soldier and lawman, taking her into the citadel.

"Here," he said, opening the lid of the strongbox and handing her the Bible. She clutched it to her chest hard enough to make Slocum a tad jealous.

"How can I thank you, John? This means so much to me. To Pierre and his memory and to me and—"

"Let's go. I've had enough of Refugio for a lifetime."

As they started out, Antoinette looked back at the treasure-laden chest.

"John . . . couldn't we . . . I mean . . . it's not ours, but it was all stolen, and they would never miss just a little of it."

"Come *on*," he said, pulling her away from the fortress. Soldiers had already been set up on the perimeter to protect what was inside. Hurrying around to the side of the fortress, he hefted saddlebags lying on the ground. Slocum mounted the horse he had stolen the night before and Antoinette had one borrowed from the cavalry. As they rode toward the pass, she let out a huge sigh again.

"We should have gotten something for our trouble."

"You have your Bible," he pointed out.

"But, well, yes, you're right."

Slocum twisted about, experiencing a twinge of pain from his damaged ribs, and opened the saddlebags on his horse. During the lull in fighting and before the cavalry arrived, he had loaded the saddlebags and heaved them over the fortress wall. They were stuffed full of greenbacks and enough gold to make it worthwhile.

"You mean you'd already . . . you took—John!"

"Race you through the pass," he called, putting his heels to his horse's flanks.

It was a dead heat to the other side, and that was just fine with both Slocum and Antoinette Thibadeaux.

Watch for

SLOCUM AND THE WATER WITCH

322nd novel in the exciting SLOCUM series
from Jove

Coming in December!